Dear Reader,

It may come as no surprise to my regular readers that I am a Christmas story superfan. When I was asked to be part of the Carey Cove Midwives "staff," I was absolutely over the moon. A Christmas nut in a beautiful seaside village? Perfection. With, of course, some emotional hurdles to leap, but my goodness, isn't it satisfying going on that journey from emotionally vulnerable to exhilarated to more vulnerable than ever, then…out there…on the horizon…is the happily-ever-after? Writing this story was a genuine pleasure. I hope you enjoy it and that it instantly makes you want hot chocolate and a candy cane. Thank you so much for being here. That is the best holiday present ever.

Xoxo *Annie O'*

CHRISTMAS WITH THE SINGLE DAD DOC

—

ANNIE O'NEIL

HARLEQUIN

MEDICAL ROMANCE

Special thanks and acknowledgment are given to Annie O'Neil for her contribution to the Carey Cove Midwives miniseries.

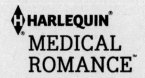

HARLEQUIN®

MEDICAL ROMANCE™

Recycling programs
for this product may
not exist in your area.

ISBN-13: 978-1-335-73744-1

Christmas with the Single Dad Doc

Copyright © 2022 by Harlequin Enterprises ULC

For questions and comments about the quality of this book, please contact us at CustomerService@Harlequin.com.

Harlequin Enterprises ULC
22 Adelaide St. West, 41st Floor
Toronto, Ontario M5H 4E3, Canada
www.Harlequin.com

Printed in U.S.A.

Annie O'Neil spent most of her childhood with her leg draped over the family rocking chair and a book in her hand. Novels, baking and writing too much teenage angst poetry ate up most of her youth. Now Annie splits her time between corralling her husband into helping her with their cows, baking, reading, barrel racing (not really!) and spending some very happy hours at her computer, writing.

Books by Annie O'Neil

Harlequin Medical Romance

The Island Clinic
The Princess and the Pediatrician

Double Miracle at St. Nicolino's Hospital
A Family Made in Rome

Dolphin Cove Vets
The Vet's Secret Son

Miracles in the Making
Risking Her Heart on the Single Dad

Christmas Under the Northern Lights
Hawaiian Medic to Rescue His Heart
New Year Kiss with His Cinderella
In Bali with the Single Dad

Visit the Author Profile page
at Harlequin.com for more titles.

To Nettybean, who has been with me
from the beginning…may it long continue!

CHAPTER ONE

'DASHING THROUGH THE…' Kiara stood back from the snowflake stencil she'd taped to the window, then gave the aerosol can a good spray. 'Snow!'

She carried on humming the Christmas song as she filled in the dozen or so other gaily shaped stencils, until her windows were transformed into magical snow crystal portals. Seeing actual drifts of snow outside her house would've made the effect even more enchanting, but the one thing Kiara wasn't in charge of in her new life here in Cornwall was the weather.

Unless…

She could dip into her Christmas Decorations Fund just a teensy bit more than she already had and buy some fake snow. Or— Ooh! A rush of excitement swept through her. A snow machine! After all, she quickly justified, any expenditure would be worth it, considering she was doing all of this mad over-the-top decorating for charity.

As a midwife, she knew just how important funding for specialised equipment was, and First Steps, her chosen charity, was renowned for helping families in need to furnish their homes with the specialised equipment they needed to give their newborn the very best chance to live a happy, healthy life. Ventilators, specialist cots, apnoea monitors… They all made the world of difference to an infant…just like being at home did.

As such, she pulled out her phone and on her increasingly long 'Christmas Decorations' list tapped in *snow machine*.

With a grin, she perched atop the armrest of her new sofa and admired her handiwork. Inside, it already looked like the day before Christmas. Stockings? Check! Chimney. Check! Tree, plate of biscuits, nativity scene, miniature glittery reindeer and unicorns? Check!

Sure, it was only the beginning of November. And, yes, she was aware of the handful of side-eyes she'd already received from some villagers, clearly wondering whether the new kid in town was a bit bonkers. She wasn't bonkers. Just new, and a bit lonely. And making the cottage feel all cosy and set for the festive season was her way of settling in. Especially as the view outside her window was no longer the familiar bustling London high street.

She twizzled round so she could look out of her new front window. Through the prisms of faux flakes she could see that outside the clear blue sky shone brightly over a crisp and increasingly autumnal Carey Cove. The leaves had turned and, courtesy of the warm afternoon sunshine, were glowing in multicoloured hues of red, orange and yellow as they floated down in colourful drifts. Not so much that the trees lay bare, but just enough to ensure there were always plenty of leaves for her to skip through if no one was around, as she went on her daily trip into the village to explore the smattering of shops along the solitary high street. Which was blissfully far away from London.

London.

The word hardened like a shard of ice in her chest. This would be the first year ever she would miss the Christmas lights being switched on. There would be no bustling into a pub after, to raise a glass of festive cheer with friends and family. No walking around the twinkling streets of London arm in arm with her boyfriend as all the shops decked their halls with boughs of—

Stop!

She didn't live there any more. Or have that life. She lived here, in the picture-post-card village of Carey Cove. A glorious sea-side village that didn't have a patch on big, old, overcrowded London, where it was far too easy to fall in love with dazzlingly talented surgeons. Surgeons who, along with having piercing blue eyes and flax-coloured hair, were *liars, liars, pants on fire*.

As if sensing the vein of discord threatening to break into her happy but still fragile new existence, her phone rang with her mum's tell-tale ringtone: a Bollywood song her mother regularly sang in an off-key, happy voice similar to Kiara's.

'Hey, Mum. Perfect timing as ever.'

'Hello, darling…' Her mum's voice instantly thickened with concern. 'Everything all right? This isn't a bad time, is it?'

'No, not at all. I meant it's just nice to hear your voice.'

And it was. Even though she was twenty-eight, and had lived on her own for years now, she was an only child, and she and her parents were very close. Her mum had stuffed countless tissues into Kiara's hands over the past ten months. Nor had she been shy about voicing her concern when Kiara had announced that moving to a different hospital in London wasn't the solution to her post-breakup blues. But a new home was.

A new home in a new village in a new county. Far, far away from London. Even her father, a poster boy for Britain's renowned stiff upper lip, had expressed concern that moving a five-hour train ride away from her family in London might not be the wisest of decisions.

'Are you all right?' her mother asked, not even pausing for breath as she added, 'It's not too late to back out, you know.'

'What?' Even the idea of leaving made her blood run cold. 'No, Mum. Honestly. I love it here. Not to mention the fact I've already signed my contract for Carey House.'

Her eyes flicked up the hill and along the treetops where, courtesy of some bare branches, she could just make out the golden stone chimney tops of the transfigured cottage hospital that commanded an arresting view of the harbour village. This was a new thing for her. Working somewhere small enough to actually learn everyone's name.

After her life had imploded last year, Kiara had felt cornered into leaving the enormous inner-city hospital where she'd worked for five years. Shame and regret had been powerful motivators. Anger, too. She'd begun what had become a long string of short-term posts in maternity wards across London, hoping to find something—*somewhere*—that would make her feel as if she was starting her life afresh. A life reboot.

She'd finally found it. Here in Carey Cove. And that was why she couldn't wait to start her new permanent midwife post at Carey House.

'I'm not backing out before I've even begun.' Kiara charged her voice with the confidence she knew her mum would be hoping to hear. 'The last thing Carey House needs is to be short-handed when all those Valentine's babies arrive.'

Her mother made a confused noise. 'I'm sorry, love. I'm not making the connection.'

Kiara grinned, perfectly able to envisage her mother's bewildered expression. 'C'mon, Mum. You know how to add. A night out on February the fourteenth with wine and flowers and romance leads to what to remember late in the month of November…?

'A baby!' Her mum laughed, but before it descended into silence she carefully began again. 'I just want to make sure you're feeling strong enough, after things with—'

Kiara cut in before her mum could bring up The Ex Who Should Not Be Named. 'All good! I love it here. And, hey…remember that charity thing I told you I set up with First Steps?'

'Oh, yes…?' Her mother said, her tone indicating that she clearly didn't remember.

Rather than mention her front garden, which was already bursting with Christmas decorations, Kiara proudly announced, 'I've got a window's worth of snowflakes.'

'Is it that cold down there?'

Kiara laughed and told her mother it wasn't. After they'd nattered a bit more, she hung up the phone, then tugged the ever-present scrunchie off her wrist and made her practised move of pulling her long hair into a swishy ebony ponytail.

She'd inherited her Indian-born, English-raised mother's jet-black hair and her British father's golden-brown eyes. Of course she missed her parents, especially near Christmas, but last year, having the carpet ripped out from underneath what she'd thought was her reality, had been quite the eye-opener. Making this change was the best thing she'd ever done.

She'd only been here in Carey Cove a fortnight, but it had been love at first scone. She looked down at her tummy and gave it a poke. Yup. Definitely a wee bit bigger than it had been. It was little wonder the Cornish were proud of their baked goods. She'd never enjoyed so many fluffy, jam-filled, clotted-cream-dolloped treats in her life. It was a good thing she was starting work tomorrow, otherwise she'd be looking a lot more like a roly-poly Mrs Claus than the too-thin version of herself who'd skulked out of London under the shadow of romantic humiliation.

She gave herself a short, sharp shake and made herself resume her off-key singing. Sure, she was single, eight weeks before her favourite time of year. And, no, it wasn't snowing…yet. But everything else in her life was firmly under her control.

As if to prove her point, she sprayed one more snowflake into place. A level of snowflake excess her ex would definitely have rolled his eyes about. So wasn't it lucky she didn't have a boyfriend to be judgemental over everything she did any more?

She put her things away and then, after tugging on her favourite bright red gilet, went out onto the small thatched-roofed porch at the front of the cottage. The estate agent had promised that in the spring it would be bedecked with graceful strands of wisteria blooms, but right now it was swathed in garlands of pine and fir and wrapped in whorls of red ribbon and fairy lights.

Unlike Carey House, which was built of large butter-coloured stones, her cottage had been painted white, with beautiful green window frames and, of course, the traditional thatched roof. It was almost impossible to believe that selling her small one-bedroomed flat in London, perched above a busy sandwich shop, had bought her this amazing picture-perfect cottage.

Memories of her ex's flat—the one she'd thought was his home—flashed through her mind's eye. Glass. Steel beams. A preponderance of grey. Barely a personal item in sight. It was so obvious to her now why she'd been buffeted with frequent refusals to let her soften the place up with some cushions and a bit of bric-a-brac.

Anyway…

That was then and *this* was the build-up to Christmas. Kiara-style.

She stepped out onto the pavement in front of the house, which stood at the end of a lane about two streets up from the harbour. One of the many things that had attracted her to both Carey Cove and Mistletoe Cottage was the fact that all the homes had a front garden. Perfect for her ever-increasing display of Christmas delights.

She scanned the decor outside her new home with an exacting gaze.

Cuckoo for Christmas…but classy?

She pulled a *Who are you kidding?* face at the nutcracker figure standing guard at her front door. Classy only because it was for charity. This was pure unabashed devotion to decorations.

So far, she had three fairy-lit deer grazing outside the small porch. She hadn't yet decided on which sleigh she wanted to harness them to…or if she wanted to get a Rudolph to attach to it. Her first instinct had been to put a sleigh on the lawn, but… One on the roof would totally be better. Maybe if she met someone at work who was taller than her—which wouldn't be hard—she could get them to help her.

Her current favourites of all the decorations were the three penguins she'd bought with her loyal customer discount at an online Christmas store. Should she get more? Or plump for the snowman who did a little jig when you pressed his button nose? Decisions, decisions!

Perhaps a little sing-song would help.

She patted the pockets of her gilet and tugged out the remote control. After a surreptitious look around—although heaven knew why she was being shy about it… she didn't exactly know anyone here—she pressed the power button.

Her insides went all tingly with childlike glee. Who didn't love a singing and dancing penguin? If there were any Scrooges around she was determined to win them over with her pure, unadulterated love of Christmas. Which reminded her… She had some huge fake candy canes she wanted to attach to the little white fence that ran along the front of her garden, leading people to the miniature Santa's Workshop donation box she'd affixed to her front gate. And those snowflake baubles. And the first of three living Christmas trees she wanted to decorate—all before she started work tomorrow.

She kept the penguins switched on while she ran into the house to get the other decorations. They would keep her company while she worked. Who knew? Tomorrow at work she might even start to make some friends who could actually talk back to her.

* * *

'Harry! Remember what I said about going too far ahead on your scooter.'

Lucas's daredevil three-year-old slowed down for about two seconds, and then… because little boys would be little boys… began to speed up again. Uphill.

Despite his concerns, Lucas laughed. He knew exactly what he'd fed his son for breakfast, and it certainly hadn't been rocket fuel. 'Harry! What's the name of the game?'

His son stopped abruptly and, with one foot on his scooter, one foot on the ground, turned round. His blond hair fell in soft curls beneath his bright red helmet. The same helmet Harry had spent the morning begging his father to refashion into a Santa's hat, even though they'd only just had Halloween.

His son's grey eyes, a reflection of his own, glittered with fun. Then he unleashed an arrestingly warm smile that could only have come from his mother, gave his father a stately salute, and pronounced, 'Safety first, Daddy.'

He smiled back, despite the sting of emotion tugging at the back of his throat as he remembered Lily's long list of things he wasn't to do once she was gone. No smothering. No over-coddling. No imposing his awareness of how fragile life could be on this little bundle of energy whose only perspective on life was that it was endless.

And, of course, the kicker: no more wearing his wedding ring after the first year.

He'd cheated. A bit. And by 'a bit' he meant an extra year and a half.

He'd taken it off when he'd been greasing up Lucas's scooter and seen that the ring was loose because he still hadn't got around to taking that Cooking Healthy Meals for your Child class the ladies at the Women's Institute kept tempting him with. The moment it had left his finger he'd realised it wasn't what connected him to his wife. His heart was. And that would be with him wherever he went, so the ring had finally gone into the keepsake box. The one his wife had started when they'd first met at uni. First cinema tickets. First airline tickets. And now first and very likely only wedding ring.

Lucas jogged up, his arms weighted with his son's all-weather coat, his backpack, his lunch, and pulled his little boy in for a hug. 'That's right, son. Safety first.'

He gave the top of Harry's helmet a loving pat and then, after giving him one more reminder about speed and distance, they set off again towards the nursery—which was, conveniently, only a hop, skip and a scooter ride from work.

Lucas stemmed another cautionary call when Harry added leaf-catching to his repertoire.

For the billionth time, man! Life isn't full of assurances. Plasters exist for a reason. Knee patches. Helmets. And doctors.

He, of all people should know that. Not just as a doctor, but as a husband. How could he forget the cancer he and his wife had convinced themselves would go into remission—

'Harry! Not too far.'

'I'm not too far, Daddy! I can still see the whiskers on your chinny-chin-chin!'

'Hey! I shaved this morning!'

Hadn't he? He put a hand up to double-check that he hadn't missed anywhere. *Struth...* He hadn't shaved. So much for being on the top of his game again. At least stubble was considered trendy. Not that his looks were a priority. His son was. Their routine. Getting their lives on a forward trajectory. And, of course, his job. The one thing besides his son that brought a smile to his face.

Since they'd relocated here to Carey Cove from Penzance, where there were far too many memories, he'd finally cracked getting their lives up and running. Morning story and cuddle in bed with his son. A shower for him while Harry played. Nursery 'uniform', such as it was, ready to be stepped into one leg at a time, then arms up overhead for the logoed sweatshirt, collar out. Hair semi-tamed into submission. Check. Check. Check.

Why had things gone wrong this morning?

Socks.

That was it.

They had a massive pile of socks and yet somehow, against the odds, there hadn't been a pair amongst them.

Note to self: buy more socks.

He had to laugh. So much for having their lives back on track. If something as simple as locating a pair of matching socks threw a spanner into their entire morning routine—

Be kind to yourself.

Another one of his wife's reminders. And, to be fair, he hadn't forgotten to shave in well over a year. Nor, as he'd done two and half years ago, had he completely given up, using what energy he had to try and soothe a crying baby whose mother would never hold him in her arms again.

'Daddy, look!' Harry pointed towards the

end of the lane where...yes...there it was. Mistletoe Cottage.

And that was when the lightbulb went on. This house—a homage to Christmas—was yet another reason his so-called 'game' was off-track right now.

The cottage all but screamed a daily reminder of the countdown to Christmas, and it was a time of year he found impossible to enjoy. Not because it had been Lily's favourite, or because it had been when they'd lost her. No. She'd lost her life in the throes of the most beautiful spring either of them had ever witnessed. It was more that Christmas was about *family*. And the most important member of their family wasn't there any more. Never would be.

And even though he'd promised himself he would make this a Christmas to remember for Harry—who, to all intents and purposes, was finally old enough to truly understand and fall head over heels in love with Christmas—he simply couldn't light that same flame of enthusiasm burning inside Harry in himself.

Thank goodness there was someone else in the seaside village who was feeling it as much as Harry. Not that they'd seen the new owner of Mistletoe Cottage yet... The

'For Sale' sign had come down a few weeks back, but it had been two weeks ago when the decorations had begun appearing. First a little Santa's house. Then a few evergreen swags. Then wreaths and baubles and a preponderance of fairy lights. Every day there was something new. Including today when... Were those *dancing penguins*?

'Penguins!' Harry crowed.

Okay. Now there were penguins. What next? Waltzing polar bears?

If Lucas had thought Harry was hot-rodding before, he'd been wrong. One sighting of the bum-wiggling penguins and his son took off, one foot madly pressing the pavement behind him, as if his life depended on it.

Lucas quickened his pace, eyes trained on his son, until something in the corner of his eye caught his attention. A woman was coming out of the front door of Mistletoe Cottage holding a box of decorations in her arms. Petite. Dark-haired. He was too far away to make out anything else.

'Aah-ow!'

Lucas's blood instantly roared in his ears. One second with his eyes off Harry and, as he'd feared, boy and scooter had parted ways.

His speed-walk turned into a run. With

the low hedge in the way, he'd lost sight of Harry. But he could see the woman's head snap back as she dropped her box of decorations on the porch and raced towards his son.

By the time he reached the cottage there were no yowls of pain. There were voices. The woman's and his son's. And then...there were *giggles*.

Harry was still on the ground, and although he'd definitely grazed his knee, he somehow seemed entirely unfazed by it. Normally there would be howling by now. But the woman crouching down, face hidden by a sheet of glossy black hair, was somehow engaged in a greeting ritual with his son.

'How do you do, Harry?' She shook his hand in a warm, but formal style. 'It's such a pleasure to meet someone who loves Christmas as much as I do.'

If she was expecting Lucas to join in the I Love Christmas Every Day of the Year Club she was obviously recruiting for, she had another think coming. It was only November. He had enough trouble mustering up excitement for the day of December the twenty-fifth.

Clearly unperturbed by his lack of response, she smiled at Harry and pointed at his grazed knee. 'Now... Important decision to make. Do you think you'd like a plaster with Santa on it? Or elves?'

'Elves!' Harry clapped his hands in delight.

The woman laughed and said she would run into the house and get some, as well as a cloth to clear away the small grass stains Lucas could see were colouring his son's little-boy knees.

Her voice had a mischievous twist to it, and underneath the bright, child-friendly exchange was a gentle kindness that softened his heart.

'I'm ever so sorry. Harry is just mad for—' Lucas began, but when she looked up and met his gaze anything else he'd planned on saying faded into nothing.

Though he knew beyond a shadow of a doubt that they'd never met, his body felt as if it had been jolted into a reality he'd always been waiting to step into. Every cell in his body was supercharged with a deep, visceral connection as their eyes caught and held. Hers were a warm brown…edging on a jewel-like amber. Her skin was beautiful, with an almost pearlescent hue. Glowing… Cheeks pink. Lips a deep red, as if they'd just received a rush of emotion.

Perhaps it was the unexpected excitement

of a three-year-old boy careering into her front garden. Perhaps it was the fresh autumnal weather. Or maybe…just maybe… she was feeling the same thing he was. A strange but electric feeling, surging through him in a way he'd never experienced before.

She blinked once. Then twice. Then, as if the moment had been entirely a fiction of his own creating, realigned her focus so that it was only on Harry. Pulling him up, dusting off some invisible specks of dust, she walked him over to the steps of her small, elaborately decorated porch and sat him down, asking if he could count how many seconds she'd be away while she ran into the house to get a plaster, and starting him off with a steady, 'One…two…three…'

She was back as Harry began to stumble over his elevens and twelves, and without so much as a glance at Lucas she turned her back and knelt down in front of his little boy. She began to clean his knee in preparation for the plaster.

Feeling weirdly blind-sided, Lucas made a lame attempt at conversation. 'Quite a display you've got here. I'm guessing you like Christmas?'

'It's for charity,' she said. 'First Steps. Do you know it?'

'I like Christmas,' Harry said.

Though Lucas couldn't see her smile, he could hear it in her voice as she answered his son. 'It's a pretty special time of year, isn't it?'

'It's when Santa comes!' Harry said.

'And who doesn't like Santa?' Lucas tacked on, feeling stupidly left out, but also completely out of his element. He wasn't into Christmas. Not at all. He wanted to make it fabulous for his boy, but…

He forced a limp smile onto his lips. The woman gave him a quick glance. It was dismissive, in the way someone might try to figure out where a fly was buzzing and then decide the fly wasn't worth her attention. Or maybe she'd seen right through him. Knew he was more *bah-humbug* than *ho-ho-ho*.

Either way, he'd definitely imagined whatever it was he thought had passed between them. It might have been electricity, but it certainly wasn't the type that led to candlelit dinners and—

Whoa!

He clearly hadn't screwed his head on straight this morning. His life was about his son and himself and making sure they were healthy and happy. End of story.

'Daddy?'

Lucas's son's expression was all the confirmation he needed that he'd definitely woken up on a side of the bed he'd never woken up on before. The cuckoo side.

'Right!' The woman stood up and briskly zipped her rather professional-looking first aid kit. 'That's you sorted, young man.'

'Say thank you to the nice…erm…' Lucas left a blank space, so that the woman could fill in her name, but no luck.

'Thank you!' Harry beamed up at her and received a warm smile and a miniature candy cane 'for later' in return.

'Have fun today,' she said, her eyes on Harry, and then, without so much as a glance at Lucas, she disappeared into her house, leaving nothing but air and mystery between them.

CHAPTER TWO

AFTER APPLYING A couple of coats of 'first day at the new job' mascara to her lashes, Kiara tugged the maroon scrunchie off her wrist and swept her hair up into a high ponytail. Her hands went through the motions intuitively, but as she got to the part when she grabbed two fistfuls of hair to cinch the ponytail tight her brain immediately flashed back to yesterday morning, when that poor little boy had crash-landed in her garden.

Though everything had happened super-quickly, she had felt as though she'd crammed an entire new relationship—highs and lows and finished—all in a matter of seconds. Somehow, when she'd come out of the house with the decorations, her scrunchie had caught on a one of the pine branches, yanking her head back, pulling her hair out of her ponytail, before she'd lurched forward to help the boy—only to look up and see that the gorgeous little boy belonged to the hottest dad in the whole world.

Deliciously chestnut-coloured hair that, despite a clean, short cut, held hints of moving round his ears and collar in the same soft curls his little boy had if he were to let it grow. Amazing grey eyes. The perfect amount of tall. She was guessing he was spot-on six foot. Anything else would require her to have a step-stool for kissing him. There had been dark shadows under those dark-lashed eyes of his. Shadows that hinted at something that might be troubling him.

But he was a dad—meaning he very likely had a wife or partner somewhere. Which, of course, made him totally off-limits for ogling, wondering how tall she'd have to be to kiss him, or imagining him wearing absolutely nothing but a Santa hat and a sprig of coyly placed mistletoe.

She'd learnt that lesson the hard way. So she'd shut down faster than Santa could put someone on the naughty list for kicking a puppy.

You'd think after what she'd been through, she would have been able to put two and two together a lot more quickly than she had. Little boy plus father equals married man.

The fact that the man was seriously hot

and had a haunted little-boy-lost lost look that made her want to make him warming winter stews set off alarm bells she couldn't ignore.

She knew exactly how things would pan out if she succumbed to one solitary, forlorn *woe is me* smile. Because she'd travelled down that path before.

I'm so lonely. All I do is pour myself into work, saving children with my incredible surgical skills, and there's no one there for me at the end of the day. Just an empty flat... with an empty bed...

Pfft. She gave herself an eye-roll, then forced herself to realign her focus on the fact that she'd both physically and emotionally moved on from the hurt and shame and, yes, the heartbreak she'd endured, and that today was the first day of the rest of her new professional life. And no matter what, it was going to be a good one.

A walk up the hill in the crisp autumn air was all Kiara needed to get those endorphins flowing again. The leaves were colourful heralds of a happy, shiny, fresh start. And why shouldn't they be? She was heading to her new job in a new village in a new nook of England, and one solitary spotting of a gorgeous dad whose adorable son clearly loved Christmas as much as she did wasn't going to throw her off her stride. No way!

When she finally reached the top of the gravelled front drive, and could soak in the full glory of her new workplace, her heart did a little jig right there in her ribcage.

Carey House could not have been a more perfect place to start her life over. There was a small general practice there, but the bulk of the hospital's business was delivering happy, healthy babies.

Helping women bring babies into the world in a cottage hospital overlooking the sea, with a gorgeous, picture-postcard village below...

Perfection.

All but skipping up to the front door, she was virtually bursting at the seams with excitement to get started.

Cheerfully wondering when—or if—the powers-that-be at Carey House would decorate the place for Christmas, she pulled open the door and saw Hazel, the warm-hearted receptionist, chatting to someone tucked just out of her line of vision in the GP's waiting room.

At the sound of the door opening Hazel turned and smiled. 'You'll be needing Nya.

Hang on a minute, love, I'll fetch her for you.'
She gave Kiara a wiggly-fingered wave, then
held a solitary finger up to indicate she'd be
over in just a moment.

Kiara grinned. She'd met Hazel Collins
when she'd come down for her interview, and
she was every bit as warm and welcoming
as Kiara remembered. The sixty-something
woman could have been a stunt double for
Mrs Claus any day of the week. She had a
beautiful billow of white hair, done up in
thick plaits and pinned atop her head, pink
cheeks, and a smile that would warm the
coldest of hearts.

Hazel claimed she had worked in the
building since it had been built. This, of
course, was patently untrue. What might
be true was the fact that her ancestors had
worked here. Formerly a large family home,
Carey House had been put together, stone by
beautiful stone, at least two hundred years
ago…if not more. It had been converted into
a cottage hospital in 1900, to help improve
maternity services in the area.

At that time, pregnant women who lived
here, or in the more remote islands off the
Cornish coast, had often struggled to find
quality medical care. These days they had
St Isolde's Hospital over in Falmouth to take

on any high-risk pregnancies or oversee un-expected complications, but with Head Mid-wife Nya Ademi in charge here at Carey Cove, suffice it to say, they delivered a lot of babies there. The vast picture wall of beau-tiful little faces was testament to that.

Kiara allowed herself to get lost in the myriad of tiny little button noses and tightly clenched eyes and teensy fingers clutching pastel-coloured swaddling until she heard Hazel approach.

'Gorgeous, aren't they?' said Kiara.

'They certainly are,' said a very male voice. One that spilled down her spine like warm caramel. One that certainly wasn't Ha-zel's.

Kiara whipped round and found herself nose to chest with Extremely Hot Dad.

A short, sharp intake of breath only made it worse. He smelled *delicious*. Like molten butter on a loaf of bread fresh out of the oven. Fresh air and—*mmm*—nutmeg.

Sweet mother of God. The man smelled like French toast in the Alps.

Her knees threatened to buckle. Her tongue turned leaden. Which was proba-bly just as well, because the first words that popped into her head were highly inappro-priate: *I'd like to climb you like a tree.*

Whatever that meant.

As it dawned on her that she was leaning in to inhale more of him she jerked back, her heart somersaulting and then lurching up into her throat. Because looking up into his face from this proximity was even better than smelling him.

He was clean-shaven today. She wasn't even sure she'd realised he'd been all rough chestnut stubble yesterday until now, when he wasn't. Would it feel good to run her fingertips along the softness of that stubble? Or would it be abrasive?

Come to think of it, how had this stranger managed to imprint himself so thoroughly on her subconscious that she was desperately trying to memorise even more of him now?

She made the mistake of looking up.

His eyes were a mesmeric grey. Like multilayered storm clouds. Each tiny sector was a different shade, demanding and receiving her full attention. Dark lashes gave them added punch. If he had been evil they would've been like little Venus flytraps, waiting to snap and snare her into his power. But something told her he wasn't evil. The tumult she saw in his eyes wasn't of his own making…it was life. And that was something she could definitely relate to.

Her gaze slipped away from his eyes, down along his nose, and landed soundly on his mouth. One of his front teeth was caught on his bottom lip—as if he, too, was struggling to figure out how to make his brain and body work together again.

Where her heart had once been, a glitter bomb had detonated. One filled with gold and starlight and warm bursts of response in her erogenous zones. Which instanly filled her with horror.

She had made a solemn promise to herself that there would be no glitter bombs detonating anywhere near her for at least a year—and *definitely* not for an insanely attractive man who was already taken.

A burning hot rage replaced the glitter bomb. This was *her* place. *Her* new sanctuary. *Her* new job. *Her* new colleagues, populating *her* new world, and despite all the precautions she'd taken to stitch her heart back together, after such an ignominious and insulting end to the love affair she had thought was real, she was keenly aware of how loose that stitching had been.

A physical ache clawed at her chest as she stepped away from him and demanded, 'What are *you* doing here?'

* * *

Lucas almost laughed. Not because Miss Mistletoe's face was full of delight or warmth or joy. More because he'd never met someone so free with their distaste of him. He couldn't exactly say he liked it, but…

Her nose crinkled in frustration as she waited for him to answer.

Crikey.

He rubbed at his jaw, perplexed to find himself in such a peculiar scenario.

He'd never seen anyone so openly repulsed at the sight of him before. And on two separate occasions. Perhaps he had a doppelgänger out there? Someone who'd caused this poor woman pain? He hoped not, for her sake, but he did kind of hope it was true for *his* sake. Because… Dammit, he didn't know why. But he wanted to get to know this woman. And the reasons were slightly too potent to explain. Particularly in this scenario.

If he were to tell her he'd had one of the most erotic dreams of his entire life last night—starring her—he imagined he would win himself a slap on the face. Deservedly so. He didn't even know her name, let alone just how soft the curves of her breasts were, or whether or not she would groan his name when he licked them and then drew her nipples into his mouth as his hands teased and…

'I'm sorry,' he began. 'I think you might be mistaking me for someone—'

'No. There's no mistake. You're you. I mean—'

She pulled her hair out of her ponytail and then swiftly re-did it, splitting her dark hair into two thick shanks and tugging it tightly into place, so that it swung from shoulder to shoulder after she'd freed it from her grasp.

His awareness of her hair, how it would feel if he ran his hands through it, was so visceral he could almost have sworn he'd done it before. Surely he must be imagining it?

His body was telling him otherwise. His fingers were twitching, as if they hungered to touch. He almost physically felt the silky strands sweep against his skin, even though she was nowhere near him. It was like a memory freshly resurfacing after having long been buried. He closed his eyes and an image passed behind his lids that should have made him blush.

She'd found her voice again, and in a crisp, clear tone he imagined would be fitting for a Victorian schoolmarm, chastising a naughty young boy who'd been pulling faces, asked,

'I meant who are you and why are you at Carey House?'

Her eyes flicked away from his before he could answer. He pounced on the free moment to scan her features—an unguarded instant to try and find something, *anything*, to divine where this open hostility had come from. But before he could find much they were back on him like golden-brown searchlights.

Even so, she had looked away long enough for him to see that her charged tone was actually fuelled by insecurity. And…worse… by fear. It made his heart clench tight for her. Never, ever would he want anyone to be frightened of him. Had it been Harry's crash? Had she— His breath caught in his throat. He hoped to God she hadn't lost a child. Losing his wife had been like being eviscerated, but losing his son… He couldn't even begin to imagine the horror.

'I'm sorry.' He held out his hand. 'I'm Lucas Wilde. The GP here at Carey House.' He pointed towards the room Hazel was just coming out of, her hands full with two plates of biscuits. 'That's the surgery in there.'

She stood there and blinked uncomprehendingly at him, as if his offering a hand to shake was the most peculiar thing she'd ever seen. What was he meant to have done? Gone in for a cheek-kiss?

'Ah! Kiara!' Hazel cut in. 'I see you've met our Dr Wilde.'

'Er…' Kiara managed.

'Oh, deary me, Dr Wilde,' Hazel chastised him warmly. 'Did you not introduce yourself to our newest midwife? This is Kiara Baxter. Kiara—this is Dr Wilde. He's our main GP here at Carey Cove.'

She carried on talking about locums, visiting GPs and the specialist doctors who sometimes came in from St Isolde's, but it all became a low buzz to Lucas, who was still trying to separate his wickedly sensual dream about a version of this woman— Kiara—from the woman who was staring at him as if she were a bull preparing to charge.

'I've just put a fresh plate of biscuits in your surgery…' He heard Hazel's voice come back into focus. 'Kiara, you're welcome to grab one from there if you like or—' She stopped herself. 'Better yet, why don't you take this plate? You're going up to the lounge, are you not? Where the lockers are? That's where you store your handbag and personal items.'

Kiara's eyes darted between the two of them as if she was trying to figure out whether or not this was some sort of joke, but then, looking down at her hands, she moved forward to accept a plate of what Lucas knew to be Hazel's secret recipe ginger biscuits.

'You'll definitely love getting your teeth into one of those,' he said, giving the side of his nose a tap and unleashing a cheesy grin.

Now Hazel was looking at him as if he had sprouted antlers as well. If he could, he'd roll his eyes. Going back to sleep and starting this day over again would be an ideal option if only the idea of going to sleep and having another one of *those* dreams was something he had any sort of control over.

They all stopped short when a cry came from just outside the building. Plates of biscuits were quickly deposited on the reception desk, and the sound of running footsteps began echoing through the corridor as Kiara raced out through the front door with Lucas quick on her heels.

A woman was virtually doubled over on the driveway, with her arms wrapped round her large, very pregnant belly.

This wasn't an infrequent occurrence on the drive of Carey House. Often Lucas found there was an ashen-faced father racing up holding a jumble of the expectant mother's handbag and overnight bag and anything else she'd demanded he bring. The staff here encouraged all expectant women to make the birth experience as personalised as they wanted. Down in his surgery he sometimes heard drifts of music coming from what he privately called 'the contractions playlists'.

Kiara had reached the woman and helped ease her back up to stand, but their conversation was too low and too far away for him to grasp.

Wait a minute.

Though he couldn't see her face, Lucas recognised the petite figure. Her stylishly cut blonde bob was masking her features, but he was sure of it now. The woman clearly in the throes of a contraction was Marnie Richards, one of the hospital's own midwives. Lucas ran across to join them.

'Hello, love. I'm a midwife here. My name's Kiara. I'm guessing you're in labour?'

'Good guess!'

Kiara laughed good-naturedly. She'd clearly been through a fair few of these tightrope walks before, Lucas thought. The kind where the expectant mother was thrilled to be having a baby but experiencing feelings she'd never had before, so was lacking her usual charm and warmth—characteristics Lucas knew

Marnie had in spades, despite her reputation as the hospital's most fastidious midwife.

'I've texted Nya—she's my midwife. Hopefully she'll figure out that I haven't quite made it indoors yet.'

'I can run in and fetch her if you like,' Lucas volunteered. 'I'm sure Kiara here would be more than happy to— Oh! Oh, dear… Another contraction?'

As Marnie let out a growl of pain Lucas took one of her hands in his and made swift introductions. And as Kiara coached her through her breathing techniques, he gave Marnie an impressed smile.

'You've got quite a grip, Marnie. I'll be picking you to be on my tug-of-war team at next year's summer party.'

Marnie laughed and said, 'Just you wait until the contractions start—oh! Coming— oof! Faster!'

'I think we might've hit that moment.' Lucas threw Kiara a pained look he hoped she'd know was for comedic effect.

She gave him a shy smile, cheeks lightly pinkened, then looked away.

As he and Kiara gently escorted Marnie, step by careful step, towards the door, Marnie huffed out her answers to Kiara's questions in short, sharp, staccatos.

Lucas caught, 'Waters broken...' 'Contractions...' and something along the lines of 'Time for this baby to enter the world now'. But perhaps not put quite as politely.

'Marnie!'

Lucas looked up to see where the new voice had come from.

Nya Ademi, the head midwife, was rushing out through the door towards them. With an apologetic smile, she nudged Lucas out of the way. 'I'm pretty sure you've got patients waiting, Dr Wilde?'

Lucas knew it wasn't a chastisement. It was Nya doing what she did best—exemplifying the Six Cs the staff at Carey House embodied. Compassion, care, competence, communication, courage and commitment.

She gave Marnie's arm a squeeze and took over the hand-holding without so much as a wince. Nya's hands must be made of steel. 'Hello, love. We didn't expect you so soon. Why didn't you ring? We don't want you having the baby out here on the drive, now, do we?'

'Ow!' howled Marnie, stopping in her tracks, trying and failing to breathe through a fresh contraction. When it had passed she gave Nya a look already tinged with fatigue. 'To be honest with you, I don't care where I have it. If I was up a tree right now, I'd have it there!'

Kiara's eyes flicked to Lucas. He shot her a questioning look. Her cheeks flushed with streaks of red. She swiftly returned her attention to Marnie.

What was that about?

A mad thought occurred to Lucas. Had she had a naughty dream about *him*? Now, that would be an interesting turn of events...

Surprise darts of heat arrowed below his belt line. The idea that she had spent some of her nocturnal hours dreaming of being tangled up in the sheets with him held appeal. Too much appeal.

He forced his concerned doctor face back into place and, spying a duffel bag a few metres back, jogged to get it.

'Up a tree? You don't want to copy that nursery rhyme, do you?' Kiara lightly teased Marnie. 'Someone's already rocked their baby on a treetop and it didn't end well. I think the Carey House birthing centre is a far more comfortable option.' Kiara counted through the breaths with her until Marnie's contraction had finished, then pointed towards the building, now only a handful of metres away. 'Let's get you inside, where we can get some monitors on you and the baby out.'

'Dr Wilde?' Hazel called from the front door. 'I'm ever so sorry, but your nine o'clock appointment is here and looking a bit anxious.'

'Be right there, Hazel. Just ensuring our number one pregnant midwife is all ticketyboo.'

'I'm perfectly all right, Lucas. Go in and see your— Sweet crumbs and empty biscuit tins!' wailed Marnie. 'No one said it would hurt like *this*!'

Kiara laughed again—a warm, inclusive laugh that said, *I hear you*. Lucas liked it. He was beginning to like a lot of things about this woman.

He opened the front door, placed Marnie's bag inside, then called to a colleague to find a wheelchair, half listening while Kiara gave Marnie some more cues on her breathing as another contraction struck when they were only a few footsteps away from the entrance.

While Marnie trained her focus on blowing slow, steadying breaths, Kiara playfully lectured her. 'As you're a midwife yourself, I'm pretty sure somewhere along the line you were warned about the pain. In fact...' she flashed Marnie a cheeky grin '… I would lay money on the fact you were.'

Kiara looked up again as Lucas ushered them in, and, for an instant he was caught in the flare of one of those genuine smiles of hers. It felt like being bathed in sunlight. Then, as if it had been an accident, and her brain had suddenly told her who she was smiling at, her attention was quickly re-diverted to Marnie. Which, he sternly reminded himself, was where it belonged.

A volley of questions ensued.

How long had Marnie been having contractions?

How many minutes in between the contractions?

Was there anyone they should ring?

'Just get me inside! I don't want to miss the window for getting an epidural.'

Kiara shot a look at Nya, who had run inside to steer the wheelchair to the door, and then to Lucas. The look spoke volumes. The window for that kind of painkiller had opened and shut a while ago.

Again, his eyes caught hers, and this time something entirely different passed between them. Trust. A shared understanding that what was happening was well within Kiara's toolbox. Not that he'd doubted it, of course—

Carey House only hired the best. But in his experience everyone began their first day at work in a new hospital in a completely personalised way. Some people—like Kiara—were clearly the 'in at the deep end' type. Others liked to observe. Some insisted on leading, to prove right off the bat that they knew their stuff. He liked where Kiara sat on the spectrum. She was comfortable with her skills and neither needed to showboat nor defer to anyone.

'Dr Wilde?' Hazel called him again, this time tapping her watch.

He ducked his head so that Marnie could see him. 'Are you three going to survive without my alpha male cheerleading?'

Marnie huffed out a laugh. 'I don't know. If it comes without painkillers maybe not!'

CHAPTER THREE

KIARA LAUGHED AS Lucas accepted Marnie's insistence that she was fine, and that he really should go and tend to his own patients now.

As schoolgirlish as she knew it was, she had to look back as he disappeared into the GP surgery. And, to her surprise, she was rewarded with another one of those soft smiles of his as he glanced back too. The kind of smile that ribboned round her heart and freed a chorus of invisible birds, singing as if it were the first day of spring and not the beginning of November.

Sweet crumbs and empty biscuit tins, indeed!

It wasn't a saying she'd heard before—and maybe Marnie had made it up, to prevent herself from swearing too much, as many mothers in labour did—but it actually suited what she was feeling. The two encounters she'd had with Lucas—her new colleague, no less—had been like delicious crumbs, strewn on a path that only led to danger. For her anyway.

Yes, he was gorgeous. And, yes, it was a bonus that he worked in the health profession—she'd learned early on in her dating 'career' that not many people understood the strange demands of a midwife's role. It wasn't as if babies worked to a schedule when they decided to appear. But those alarm bells had rung for a reason when their paths had all but literally collided yesterday. Lucas Wilde was a father. And where there were fathers there were usually mothers. And mothers very rightly didn't like it when their husbands wove them a tale of deception in order to woo a twenty-something midwife who thought she might be starting a family of her own one day…

Nya's steady voice pulled her attention back to where it needed to be. On Marnie.

'That's right, love. Let's get you in here and pull off some of these layers before— Oh! Easy, there, darling… Kiara, do you think you could help Marnie get her things off while I run and let the desk know we're here and ready for action?'

'Absolutely,' Kiara said, guiding Marnie

over to the bed. 'Why don't we get your coat off? Then you can have a seat and I'll help you with everything else.'

'None of it's gone according to plan!' Marnie panted. 'I have lists. I have charts. I do this for a *living*! I thought I was the one in control.'

We all think we're the one in control.

Kiara stemmed the quip. It wasn't what Marnie needed or wanted to hear. It also referred to a dark mark on her own past that she wanted to leave behind. Which was exactly why she needed to remember to give Lucas the cold shoulder whenever their paths crossed again. But smiling at him was so easy! She hadn't noticed yesterday that there was a twinkle in his eyes when he tried to be funny. How he could make dad jokes sexy was beyond her. Dad jokes should never be sexy. Especially to her.

She knelt down and got to work on Marnie's winter footwear. 'That's right…just sit back against that big, snowy mound of pillows while I get these boots off for you.'

'Sorry about all the laces,' Marnie apologised. 'Again—not part of the plan.'

Kiara smiled up at her before putting both the boots in a small cupboard ready for the expectant mother's personal items. 'It'd be great if babies listened when we told them the plan, wouldn't it?'

Marnie laughed appreciatively. She gave her belly an affectionate rub. 'I was out for a walk. I thought it'd be good for the baby and my swollen ankles if I had some gentle exercise. I had my first contraction when I was out on the beach, but I thought it was a Braxton Hicks so decided to ignore it. If I'd known it was the real thing I would've worn some slip-ons.'

Marnie gave a self-deprecating chuckle, then sighed.

'Heaven knows why I thought I'd be the one in charge of all this.' She pointed at her stomach, and for just a moment her smile shadowed as she said, 'I guess it's because I'm the one who organised this whole scenario. Her,' she corrected herself, her smile warming again. 'She's not a scenario. She's a her.'

'Oh?' Kiara said, keeping her tone light, but neutral.

She'd learnt hundreds of babies ago that it was always best to leave the baby's origin story to the mum to tell. Not every family came pre-packaged with a fairy tale romance, a diamond ring and a baby nine months after the honeymoon.

Another contraction hit before Marnie could explain, but once it had passed, and Kiara had got Marnie out of her clothes and into one of the soft hospital gowns, she glanced at the empty chair usually occupied by the birth partner and thought it was safe to ask, 'You didn't say before, but is there anyone you'd like me to ring?'

Marnie's cheeks coloured. 'No,' she answered curtly, and then, her forehead creasing apologetically, added, 'Sorry. Sorry... I'm pregnant on my own through IVF treatment—which most people already know. I haven't had to explain how I got to look like a beached whale without having a boyfriend in a while.'

'You just let me know what I can do to help, okay?'

Kiara meant it, too. Having a baby was a big step. Having it on your own was even bigger. It took courage to do what Marnie was doing and she definitely wasn't judging. Everyone's path was of their own making, and Marnie's voice was rock-solid. She wanted a baby and now she was having one. Exactly the same way Kiara wanted to celebrate this Christmas with complete and utter abandon.

Okay, fine... It was a little bit different.

But the endgame was the same. She and Marnie were living their lives by their own rulebooks. And she respected that.

Kiara silently began hooking Marnie up to the relevant monitors, making it clear that it was up to Marnie how much she did or didn't say.

'Do you mind if I take a little look,' she asked eventually. 'See how far along you are?'

'Please,' Marnie said. 'I'd do it myself, but…' she pointed at her large belly '…this is in the way.'

Kiara glanced at the door, certain that Nya would be reappearing any minute. 'I know you work here, but I think that if there was a day of all days when Nya would be happy for you to sit back and let someone else do the work, today would definitely be the day.'

The women shared a warm smile. And Kiara thought she'd look forward to working with Marnie when her maternity leave was finished.

'Nya's probably got stuck at the desk answering four million questions. If you want to take over for her, please feel free.'

'Are you sure? If she's your midwife—'

Marnie gave a combination of a laugh and a moan. 'When you work as a midwife *everyone's* your midwife.' Her smile softened. 'Nya has been the one to do all the exams, but it's shift-change time, so honestly… Oh!' Her hands flew to her belly. 'You can go ahead. Please.'

'Right you are, then. But if you want me to step aside for Nya, just say.'

Kiara gloved up, put some gel on her hand and pulled a stool over so she could do a quick examination.

Rather than flinch, as many patients did at the first touch, Marnie suddenly beamed a big, huge, beautiful smile. 'I'm going to be the mother of a little baby girl!'

'You are!' Kiara beamed back. 'And…' she finished her examination '…by the looks of things, you'll be holding her in your arms and picking out the perfect name any minute now.'

'Sorry…sorry!' Nya appeared at the door, her smile mischievous as she briskly walked to the wall-mounted glove dispenser. 'A woman having twins cornered me on the way here, but I knew I'd left you in capable hands.' She gave Marnie a discerning look. 'You're choosing names already, are you?'

Marnie nodded and then, as a contraction hit again, somehow managed to get out, 'I

know—I haven't—physically experienced—
this—before—but I'm pretty sure—'

'You're crowning!' Nya and Kiara cho-
rused in tandem.

At Marnie's request, Nya took on the
hand-holding role. Then, after two, possibly
three minutes of encouragement, some deep
guttural cries and some concentrated pushing later, Kiara was holding Marnie's baby
girl in her arms.

'She's a beauty!' Kiara held her up so Marnie could see, and as if on cue the little girl
uttered a loud cry, announcing her arrival
in the world.

They all laughed and, exhausted, Marnie
fell back against her pillows.

Nya and Kiara cleaned and dried the baby,
then placed her in Marnie's outstretched arms
so that they could share that all-important
skin-to-skin contact both mother and baby
craved organically.

Kiara was relieved at how easy it had been
to fall into a rhythm with Nya who, despite
being her boss, was treating her as an equal,
only taking the lead when it came to finding things—which, to be fair, was something
Kiara did need guidance with.

'Nothing like starting your first day with a

baby born in the first ten minutes,' she said, and grinned.

Nya shared a complicit smile with her. 'It's the best way to start a new post, isn't it? One perfect baby on a beautiful day.'

Nya prepared a Vitamin K injection and Marnie reluctantly handed her little girl over to Kiara for weighing and measuring. They dealt swiftly with the umbilical cord and the placenta, offering Marnie a local anaesthetic for the inevitable pain she felt, and finally moved the new mother and her freshly swaddled daughter to a bright, clean bed.

'I can see why new mums sometimes get teary at this part,' Marnie said, blinking back her own tears.

Kiara gave her a warm smile. 'There are a billion hormones running rampant in your body right now,' she told her. And she was also alone. There was no one special to share this life-changing moment with.

She pictured this moment for herself. Her brain summoned the images and she was shocked to see that Lucas was the one standing in the room next to her—not her ex, Peter. It wasn't so much a clear image of Lucas as a doting father, but more his presence she imagined. That calm, warm, humour-filled aura that had surrounded him

from the moment they'd discovered Marnie
on the driveway.

'I know…' Marnie sniffed, already holding
out her arms for her baby again. 'I've known
all that professionally for years, but now I
feel like I truly *know* it. In here.' She tapped
her heart. 'I don't know how she's done it,
but this little girl has made me complete. I
feel like I've just become the person I was
always meant to be.'

Kiara smiled, but said nothing, knowing that her voice would squeak up into the
higher registers if she did. She knew the feeling of knowing there was something missing
in her life…not yet having it. She also knew
that the sense of wholeness had to come from
within. That more than likely whatever had
led Marnie to go through IVF and have this
baby alone had been a step in the process of
recognising and owning the type of woman
she wanted to be.

Kiara wanted to be a woman who could
trust and love a man again. She wasn't going
to tar all men with the same brush her ex had
been lavished with, but…

Again, an image of Lucas flashed up in
her mind's eye.

She tried to bat it away but it wouldn't go.

This was insane. She'd barely met the man.

And yet just a few moments in his presence and she'd known instinctively that he was someone she could rely on. Professionally. Obviously. Just because looking at him set butterflies loose in her tummy, it didn't mean she couldn't take a step back and acknowledge that, at her place of work, he was a good man to know.

The thought snagged.

Having a doctor's respect meant a lot to her. Perhaps that was why she'd been so smitten by her surgeon boyfriend. A surgeon dating a midwife... It was so clichéd. But that first time Peter had asked her opinion about something and nodded along, as if she'd just offered him the most valuable insight ever, had thrilled her. The 'respect' had turned out to be just for show, of course. Peter had only ever valued Peter's opinion.

But with Lucas the respect had seemed genuine. The man had surely delivered a few babies over the course of his training, if not during his career as a GP, and he had seemed completely at ease leaving Marnie's care to Kiara. She hadn't got the impression from him—even for a nano-second—that he considered her less than capable of looking after her patient. She respected him for that.

And it spoke of the self-confidence he possessed that he hadn't felt the need to micro-manage her—a stranger whose skills were completely unknown to him. A stranger who had kind of been a little bit rude to him, now that she thought of it. She'd been warm and kind to his son, but she'd been crisp and dismissive of him…right up until they'd shared *that* look. The one that had turned her insides into a warm cupcake.

'Are you all right, Kiara?' asked Marnie.

Kiara shook her head, as if that would shake away the image of Lucas now firmly embossed in her brain. 'I'm just really delighted that your baby was the first one I helped to deliver,' she said.

'You and Lucas saved me from having her outside!' Marnie laughed, then gave a sigh that was difficult to read. 'Have you had a chance to chat with him yet?'

Kiara shook her head, even though it wasn't strictly true. He had tried to chat, but she'd shut it down.

'He's such a good man,' Marnie continued. 'Not everyone would be as kind and thoughtful as he is, given his situation.'

Kiara's eyebrows drew together. 'What situation?'

Marnie's eyes darted to the open door, then back to Kiara. 'It's not really my place to say, but a good man like that deserves to meet someone really special.'

Like me?

Marnie was making poor work of stifling a yawn.

'Why don't you have a rest?' Kiara helped Marnie arrange her covers and pillows just so, unable to stop her smile twitching into something broad, as if she'd just received the best Christmas present ever.

Lucas Wilde wasn't married!

She tried to pull her smile into some sort of control. Boyfriend-shopping was not on her list of things to achieve here. Delivering babies and decorating her house to collect money for charity were. And looking after herself. That was it.

Even so…just a handful of minutes with Lucas today had shown her a side of him that she really liked. Beyond the sexy hair, the beautiful grey eyes and those lips that really did look inviting enough to kiss…

A good man like that deserves to meet someone really special.

An image of her wearing a sexy elf costume, one leg wrapped seductively round a giant candy cane, popped into her head. And Lucas was wearing nothing more than a Santa hat…

Kiara! Stop it. He's a single father, not a boy toy.

She wrapped things up with Marnie, who looked more than ready for a sleep, especially now that her daughter had nodded off, and headed down to the central desk to do her notes.

'Well, that's a new way to approach the desk!' Nya smiled as she approached. 'It's not often someone skips to come and do their notes.'

'Was I skipping?' Kiara hadn't even noticed. The Lucas Effect? 'It was a great delivery,' she said. 'Always gives me a boost.'

'You're certainly in the right job if delivering babies gives you added pep!' Nya gave her arm a squeeze, then showed her where to do her notes, telling her the two of them would soon sit down to discuss her future patients.

Kiara started filling out her forms, but she couldn't stop her mind from wandering just a bit. Had Lucas Wilde really made her *skip*?

Sure, he was great. But finding out he was single couldn't be the main reason she was so happy. She'd already had a three-year run at having a man as the centre of her universe. It had blown up in her face in spectacular style. And that was the thing she needed to remember. Along with the fact that perhaps she didn't need to be quite as cool a customer when it came to a certain Dr Wilde...

Lucas scanned his patient's test results, together with the symptoms she'd described, and gave her the information he knew she didn't want to hear. 'I'm afraid you have entered the phase of life known as perimenopause, Mrs Braxton.'

'Oh, please...' The forty-seven-year-old woman batted away his formal address, reaching for one of the tissues out of the box Lucas had extended to her. 'Call me Becky. Everyone else does, and it's the one thing that still makes me feel young. Well...that and my thirty-something boyfriend.' She threw him a watery smile, dabbed away a few tears, then blew her nose, sitting back in her chair with a sigh. 'It was a bit mad thinking I still might be...you know...'

Lucas did know, but he thought it best to let Becky say the words herself.

'Able to have a baby. At my age.'

He held out the tissue box again. 'It isn't an impossibility, but I will caution you—'

'That pregnancy at my age comes with added risk.' She threw her hands up and gave a tearful laugh. 'I know. Down's. High blood pressure. Gestational diabetes.'

'There are risks for both you and the baby, so if you are sexually active and still trying for a child it's worth remembering the possible risks that could arise from a geriatric pregnancy—'

'Oh, God! Let me stop you there.' She repeated the words *geriatric pregnancy* with a tone of pure horror. 'It just sounds so... so...*old.*'

'Eighty-eight is old,' Lucas said with a gentle smile. 'A hundred and three is old. And, for the record, I have seen patients of both ages earlier this morning—both of whom, I am happy to report, are fit and well despite their additional life experience.'

Lucas hoped his smile would say what propriety wouldn't allow him to. Becky Braxton was an attractive, intelligent woman, who was clearly in a happy, healthy sexual relationship with a younger partner who adored her, seeing as he'd texted three times already during her visit.

Children might not be on the cards for her, but that didn't mean she had to buy herself a wheelchair and consider her life over and done with.

He tapped the test results he'd just printed

out. 'You are healthy and fit. Those are valuable assets.'

He was about to say she would have de-
cades of other experiences ahead of her, but
he knew first hand that life didn't always
work out like that. So he gave her a couple of
pamphlets and said he was more than happy
to talk through some of the physical changes
she could expect over the coming years, or
offer a referral if she preferred to discuss it
with a woman doctor.

'Heavens, no!' Becky pooh-poohed the
idea. 'You're ever so kind, but I suppose…
Oh, I do hate to be personal, but when I heard
about your situation, and saw you were getting on with your life, I thought, *If young,
handsome Dr Wilde can take one of life's
more serious blows on the chin and pick himself and get on with it…so can I.*' She pressed
her fingers to her mouth, then let them drop
into her lap, her expression anxious. 'I hope
that isn't too intrusive? It's just—you know—
it's a small village, and people know things
about people here. In a friendly way.'

'I know,' he said. 'It's a very welcoming
place.'

More than enough stews and casseroles
had been left on his front porch when he'd
first moved in, to make it clear that life in

Carey Cove was about being part of a community. Not hiding away and licking his wounds as he had back in Penzance, when he'd been not even thirty, the father of a six-month-old son and newly widowed.

He'd learnt the hard way that life after a bereavement was not about forgetting—because how could you forget someone you'd promised to love till death parted you? You couldn't. Nor could you stop loving them. Especially when you woke up to a three-year-old version of that person every single morning.

'How do you do it?' Becky asked. 'Get on with life when it's not going to be remotely like the one you thought you'd be living?'

'Good question,' he said, doing his best to lean into the question rather than avoid it. People came to their GP when they were feeling vulnerable. Frightened. He knew he couldn't give her a perfect answer, but he could explain what he'd done. 'For me and Harry—my little lad—it was finding a way to live with our new reality. It was less difficult for him, of course, but—'

'I'm sorry,' Becky cut in. 'That was extremely personal of me. I suspect I need to go home, have a bit of sulk and a think, and then just get on with it. That's what we British do, isn't it?'

'As long as you're not letting anything fester,' Lucas said, meaning it.

He'd known that if he'd stayed in the house he and Lily had thought was to be their 'for ever' home he'd have been tending wounds that would never heal. The move here had felt like a physical necessity.

'If you need a referral to talk to someone, or would like some phone numbers of charities, I'm happy to pass them on.'

A thought caught and snagged his attention. He didn't know what it was, but something told him Kiara's move to Carey Cove had been for exactly the same reason his had. To give herself a clean slate. A fresh start.

Losing his wife had been a gut-wrenching loss, but he'd at least been able to pour his love into their son, ensuring that Harry felt as safe, happy and secure as they had wanted all their children to feel—*their child*, he silently corrected. Because there wouldn't be more children, would there? Not without falling in love again, trusting his heart again. Taking the risk of stepping off the edge of a cliff and believing, once again, that this time he would actually get to spend the rest of his life loving and caring for someone who felt the same way about him.

He stemmed the thought.

Once in a lifetime had been a blessing.

Harry was a blessing.

Kiara was just—

Wait. What? Kiara wasn't meant to have entered that particular thought process. Particularly when he was thinking about falling in love again.

He realigned his focus to where it should be. On his patient. 'Have you considered adoption? Fostering?'

She shook her head. 'No, not really.' She grabbed another tissue, dabbed her eyes clear of mascara, and popped on her usual bright smile. 'Anyway, it's simply too embarrassing, sobbing my heart out in front of you. I'll figure something out.' She gave his hand a pat, as if their roles had suddenly been reversed and she was the one consoling him. 'Thank you, Dr Wilde. No disrespect, but I hope our paths don't cross again too soon. Unless—' her smile genuinely brightened this time '—it's down at the harbour? They're turning on the Christmas lights tomorrow night. Your little one might like that. It's always such a lovely evening. Mulled wine, mince pies, and of course all the lights.'

'That sounds wonderful.'

Lucas saw her out of the surgery and as it was now lunchtime thought he'd pop upstairs to the room Nya had told him Marnie was in. He'd rung earlier, to see how the labour had gone, and had been delighted to hear she'd delivered her healthy little girl in record time.

A few minutes later, he was just about to enter the room when Kiara came out, chart in hand. Her eyes brightened at the sight of him. It was a nice change from the cool reception he'd been given the first couple of times their paths had crossed. Perhaps he'd surprised her, or caught her out... Who knew? There were a million reasons why someone's initial encounters with another person might not be perfect.

'I take it she's sleeping?' Lucas said in a low voice.

Kiara's dark brown eyes flicked back towards the bed. She nodded, and gently pulled the door shut behind her. 'Like a baby,' she said. '*With* her baby,' she added with a soft laugh, her gaze dipping and then lifting to meet his.

Something hot and bright flared between them, causing them both to look away. There was something both of them were shy of,

Lucas thought. Was it something neither of them had expected or wanted?

It was a question he couldn't answer.

'How are you getting on?' He gave a teasing glance at his watch. 'What's it been? Four hours? Delivered any more babies?'

Kiara shot him a shy grin. 'Not yet. Although there have been a couple more December babies added to my roster, so I'll definitely be looking forward to swaddling them in seasonal blankets.'

Lucas threw her a questioning look.

Kiara led him over to the supplies cupboard and pointed to a couple of fresh stacks of swaddling blankets with a variety of patterns: Santas, elves, holly and ivy, even bright red reindeers in a Nordic design.

'I didn't even realise we had seasonal swaddling,' Lucas said.

Kiara flushed and admitted, 'That would be my fault.'

'How?'

'Back in the hospital where I used to work, we would sometimes get samples from companies wanting to sell these. When I knew I'd be moving here at Christmas time I contacted one of the suppliers to see if there were any samples available, and they sent this huge box full. They're last year's designs, so...'

'So Carey House is the lucky recipient?' Lucas said. 'I'm impressed. You're not just a fan of Christmas at home, you spread the joy.'

Again, her gaze dropped, then lifted to meet his. The compliment—however generic—had obviously touched her. Her response, lightly pinkened cheeks and a tooth snagging on her lower lip, made his heart skip a beat.

Something—or more likely someone— had hurt this woman. Made her feel less valued than she should be.

'Well...' Kiara finally broke the silence. 'I wanted to do something to show how appreciative I am of being taken on as part of the team here.'

'Christmas swaddling blankets was a nice choice,' Lucas said, and then, because he couldn't help himself, asked, 'You worked in London before, right?'

Kiara let out a low whistle. 'Word travels fast in these parts.'

Lucas gave her a knowing grin. 'Tell me about it. When I moved here—'

He stopped himself. He wasn't ready to bring up the cancer, the months of praying that this time, this check-up, his wife would get the all-clear.

He began again. 'When I moved here, I received a very warm welcome. There are fewer folk to spread the news to, I guess. Fewer than up in London, anyway.'

The expression on Kiara's face suggested to him that she'd seen the dark shadows flit through his eyes when he referenced his move. Or perhaps she'd read him like a book the moment she'd met him. Seen the light blue shadows that had taken up residence under his eyes in those last heartbreaking days of Lily's life and refused to leave. Sensed the void in his life he didn't know how to fill or what or who to fill it with.

But instead of trying to prise more information out of him, Kiara volunteered, 'I worked at London Central.'

Lucas looked impressed. 'You'd certainly get your daily steps in at that place. I mean—' He stopped, smacking himself on the forehead with the heel of his hand. 'Not that you need to count steps. Midwives are some of the most active people I've ever met, and you're obviously very fit and slender and—' He was about to say *beautiful*, but something stopped him, so he faked a cough and asked, 'Did you enjoy your time there?'

Kiara quite happily pretended she hadn't noticed his weird gaffe. She was obviously private, too, but she did volunteer, 'It was amazing. I started there straight out of university, and it was trial by fire, really. But the care there is much more doctor-led. Not to diminish what you do—obviously it's super-important. But I guess before I did the job I had imagined that being a midwife would be more like it has been here from the moment I arrived.'

Lucas felt himself caught in her enthusiasm. The warm glow of her smile. 'You mean pregnant women appearing on the driveway about to give birth?'

Kiara shot him a cheeky grin. 'If she'd been riding a donkey and had a man in hessian robes alongside her it would've been even better.'

He gave her a disbelieving look.

'No!' She was laughing as she waved the nativity image away. 'I was obviously delighted we got to Marnie in time, and that we didn't have to worry about there being no room at the inn. It was more… Well, you, for example. You saw that the midwives had things under control and honoured the fact that it's our area of expertise.'

'But it *is* your area of expertise.' Lucas felt

he was missing something here. 'That's the point of midwifery.'

'I know!' Kiara laughed and clapped her hands. 'Exactly. It's just…lots of times in the London hospital there were incidents when male obstetricians would elbow us aside although we were perfectly capable of handling the situation. Women helping women, you know?'

Lucas scanned her expression, looking for something that might signal that she disliked or mistrusted men in general, but found nothing. Maybe there'd been a bully in her department? Or perhaps it was simpler than that? Perhaps she was referencing the traditional customs of childbirth that went back much further than modern medicine did?

Kiara must've sensed that she needed to explain herself a bit more, so she continued, 'I like being a woman's wingman. And her partner's—if there is one,' she added hastily, with a quick glance towards Marnie's room. 'Being with her almost from the beginning as she rides the world's most exhilarating and terrifying rollercoaster of all. Bringing someone new into the world…'

Her passion spoke to him. It was akin

to his love of being a GP. Helping people throughout the various stages of their lives.

'You look like someone who loves her job very much,' he said.

'I do. I love it. Absolutely. And I just know I'm going to love it here too.'

Her eyes shone bright. To the point where Lucas knew he'd be caught in their brilliance for longer than was appropriate. So again he resorted to the fake cough manoeuvre and excused himself.

He was responding to Kiara in ways he'd never thought he'd experience with a woman again. Curious to know more. Wanting to be around her. Hyper-aware of himself when he was. And that wasn't even counting the starring role she'd had in the erotic dream he'd had last night.

It scared him. He and Harry had only just got themselves into a steady, workable routine. He wasn't sure he had it in his emotional toolbox to change things yet again. Not in this way.

He could feel her eyes on him as he left the ward…and for the first time in years he liked knowing that someone was looking.

He kept his pace slow and steady—and then, when he hit the stairs, surprised himself by hoisting his bum cheek up onto the banister and sliding all the way down.

When he got to the bottom, he was smiling.

And so was Nya, who'd seen the entire thing.

CHAPTER FOUR

Just as she was about to do her first lash, Kiara gave her mascara wand the side-eye and then, after one long hard stare, set it back down. She wasn't going to dress up for her second day at work, and she definitely wasn't dressing up for Dr Lucas Wilde. Even if he did make her skip along the corridor at work and think surprisingly saucy thoughts as she slipped into bed.

Even so, when she went out to her front garden—coat on, backpack loaded and ready to go to work—she found herself accidentally on purpose dawdling. Changing the angle of the dancing penguins by a smidge. Realigning a couple of waist-high candy canes that were listing ever so slightly in the crisp breeze coming in straight off the sea.

She had all the lights on already. With the mornings dark for so long, she thought it might be fun for the hardworking fishermen to look back to the coast and be able to spot her home, shining bright like a Christmas lighthouse, welcoming them back to the beautiful little harbour below when they brought in the morning's catch.

She turned and looked out to sea, just making out the skidding movement of white horses atop the waves. When she turned back around, the twinkling delights of her decorated cottage hit her afresh. It looked like a real-life gingerbread house. One that was hosting visitors from all over the North Pole. She tapped the black nose of the polar bear she'd set up last night after work. He was standing guard over a pile of 'presents'— colourfully decorated weatherproof boxes, arranged in an artful tumble and coming out of a huge Santa sack.

She'd checked with the neighbours first, assuring them that she wouldn't have the house flashing and blinking like a Vegas casino, and had been thrilled to discover they were all collectively delighted with her efforts. They'd even pledged to donate to First Steps in the name of Mistletoe Cottage.

It wasn't the glory she was after...it was knowing that something she'd done would be bringing care and solace to families unable to afford medical equipment for their poorly newborns. Life was hard enough when you brought a child into the world. Having medical problems to take on board when your finances were tight was even worse.

She shouldered her backpack, locked the front door, and gave her home an appraising look. It looked spectacular. If you loved Christmas, that was.

Her gaze drifted down the lane to where she had first seen Lucas and Harry, but it was completely devoid of human life. Just a few leaves scudding across the pavement.

A strange feeling of emptiness threatened to nibble away at the glow of anticipation she'd woken up with. She'd practically bounded out of bed. And it wasn't just the joy of going to work at Carey House she'd been looking forward to. It was the giddy sense of excitement about who she was going to see at Carey House. Today, she'd vowed silently, she would be less wary of Lucas Wilde and more...

Hmm... She'd have to work on that part, because obviously pouncing on the man and kissing him was out of the question. No. That sort of 'staff Christmas party' behaviour was not going to be a part of her strategy. As if she were as calculated as that. She wasn't. Not in the slightest. What she really needed here in her new home was a friend. Independent of her attraction to him, Lucas Wilde seemed like excellent friend material. And also a very, *very* sexy dad.

A sound at the end of the lane caught her attention. As if thinking about his father had magicked him into appearing, a familiar looking blond boy, kitted out in a red woolly hat and a matching puffer jacket, came careering round the corner, one foot madly pushing away at the pavement that stood between him and her increasingly over-the-top Christmas display.

Her heart softened.

Harry.

With or without the sexy dad he was a darling little boy. Precocious. Full of beans. And clearly as in love with Christmas as she was.

'Morning, Harry! Remember to slow down for the corner— Oops! There you are. Nice one. You're getting better at stopping, aren't you?'

'Penguins!' he cried, as the timer she'd set clicked into action.

She gave him a complicit grin and read-justed his knitted hat as he leant his scooter against the fence. 'Want to take a closer look?'

Wide-eyed with a combination of disbelief and pleasure, he looked up at her, his big grey eyes a carbon copy of his father's. 'Yes, please.'

'Well, go on, then. They were asking for you this morning.'

'They were?' Harry's eyes grew even bigger.

'Absolutely.' She put on a funny voice she hoped sounded like a penguin. '"When's Harry coming over for a dance?"'

Harry needed no further encouragement.

'Good morning, Kiara.'

Lucas's butter-rich voice all but physically pulled her up to stand. When she met his gaze, she was delighted to see it was matched with a smile. Less dubious than it had been yesterday at Carey House. There was warmth in it. Comfort. And, if she wasn't mistaken, a hint of that same fizz of anticipation she knew was glittering in her own eyes. They held one another's gazes for a moment, the atmosphere between them teetering on the precipice of too nice for Kiara to be able to resist and…*uh-oh*…blushing.

'Morning.' She feigned a crucial readjustment to her bobble hat and pointed to the lane. 'Off to work?'

Of course he is, you idiot! He's not heading to the zoo.

Lucas nodded, his eyes skidding from one decorative tableau to the next. 'And to the childminder's. Harry insisted we left early enough to visit The Christmas Lady.'

His face became less easy to read. Though he was obviously trying to fulfil his son's wishes, something about her or Christmas wasn't letting his smile reach his eyes.

'Are you not a fan of Christmas?' she blurted, instantly regretting it when he winced.

'Is it that obvious?' He waved the words away. 'That's not exactly the case. It's more—' His phone beeped and he pulled it out. The wince turned into a frown. 'Sorry. We've got to get going.' He took in her hat, the bag on her shoulder and the winter coat as if seeing her for the first time. 'Want to join us?'

Yes. Absolutely, she did. But if this was precious father-son time she didn't want to intrude. 'If you're sure...?'

Lucas's smile was genuine now. 'I am. Sorry. It's just—' He did a quick scan of her house and called Harry over with a loving, 'Time to go now, son.' Then, 'I don't have the best relationship with Christmas, and as this is the first one this little monkey is going to properly remember I'm trying to plumb some of the Christmas spirit by proxy.'

Kiara took this as her cue. 'You want

Christmas spirit by proxy? I can do that. In spades.' She gave him a little salute. 'Christmas spirit by proxy, at your service!'

Lucas gave a good-natured laugh and then, to her surprise, reached out and gave her candy-cane-striped scarf a little tug. 'If it's anything like your midwifery I'm sure you'll be an excellent guide.'

Her blush deepened. 'You hardly saw me do anything.'

'I saw enough to know that you're good at your job. And, perhaps more importantly, that you love it. Have you had any updates on your patient?'

She pulled out her phone and thumbed up the photo she'd asked one of the night nurses to send her. Marnie and her baby nuzzling one another's noses. It was a really sweet photo, and unexpectedly tugged at a longing she didn't dare give voice to. She was around babies every single day and had never before had this response to a mother-baby moment. Not even with her ex. What had changed?

'Hold it up a bit?' Lucas was asking, putting his hand under hers to bring it to his eyeline.

Again, that twist of longing swept through her, but this time it came with glittery sparks of delight whooshing through her bloodstream. Sparks that had absolutely nothing to do with the tall, dark and handsome doctor with a snowman backpack hanging from his arm, leaning into her personal space to look at the photo.

God, he smelled good.

This morning he was more like vanilla latte with hints of cornflakes and berries than the sexy woodcutter aroma he'd left in his wake yesterday. Not that she'd be smelling him every time their paths crossed. Much. But that was hardly her fault. He was like the scented version of a kaleidoscope.

When he pulled back, she instantly missed his proximity. She'd never known lust at first sight to be so potent.

'They look well. I'll have to check in on them today,' Lucas said, mercifully having missed the twist of her features as she took a final look at the photo and then closed it down.

She wasn't jealous of Marnie. She was happy for her. Though she hadn't yet heard her whole story, Marnie seemed a picture of contentment...just her and her baby.

Kiara had always pictured something different for herself. Something like what her parents shared. A happy, solid friendship that had led to a loving marriage. They'd had their ups and downs through the years—she was beginning to learn there weren't many couples who enjoyed entirely smooth sailing once they vowed to spend a lifetime together—but they had always dealt with their problems together. As a family. She admired them for that, and knew that her ideal relationship would contain those core principles of love and respect.

'So...' Lucas began after they'd walked in silence for a bit. 'Do you always decorate for Christmas like this?'

She barked a laugh. 'No. This is new. I don't think the rest of the tenants in my building in London would have taken to me turning their homes into a great big flashing Christmas orgasm. Oh, God!' She clapped her hands over her mouth. 'I'm sorry. I don't know what made me describe it that way. Especially in front of your son—' She squeezed her eyes tight in humiliation. 'I'm making this worse. Much, much worse. The more I talk, the worse it gets. Please save me from myself!'

Lucas, to her relief, was laughing rather than looking horrified. He lowered his voice and, as if they were sharing a secret, leant in and intoned, 'Maybe in future you could use the phrase "festive wonderland" when Harry's within earshot?'

Her cheeks burnt with embarrassment. 'I am so sorry. I'm not really getting off on the right foot as your number one Christmas spirit guide, am I?'

He shook his head, but didn't look annoyed or even put off by her series of verbal gaffes. 'This is the childminder's.'

She stood back as the carer came out of her lovely rambling home, tucking a well-loved cardigan around herself as she greeted them with the news that the children would be having a biscuit-making party after lunch today.

Harry cheered, then waved to Kiara. 'I'll make you a Santa biscuit!'

She grinned, and pressed her hands to her heart in thanks. She looked across at Lucas, whose expression had suddenly gone blank. Unreadable. He seemed to be actively avoiding eye contact with her.

Had she done something wrong?

He knelt down in front of Harry and gave him loving but stern reminders to wear his coat when he was playing outdoors and to listen to the childminder—especially when she said it was time for a nap. He gave him a kiss on the forehead and tugged one of the little blond curls peeking out from under his hat. And then, as if it had suddenly become physically painful for him to leave his little boy, he briskly rose, turned, and walked back out to the pavement, where he instantly set off at a clip.

Kiara wasn't sure what had just happened. Was that sort of a goodbye normal for them? Maybe it had been a bit stiff because she'd been watching. Or was it because Harry had offered to make a biscuit for her?

This and a thousand other questions clamoured for supremacy as she jogged up to him and, in as light a tone as possible, asked, 'Are you upset that you're not going to get to go to the biscuit-making party? I get it. I love making and decorating biscuits—all those hundreds and thousands...'

He stopped and threw her a look saturated with sadness. His grief was so pure, so undiluted, it tore her own heart open with compassion. Whatever was haunting this man was big. Well beyond anything she'd endured. And that wasn't slighting what she'd been through at all.

It had been life-changing. And not in a good way.

But it had led her here...

'I really want to give Harry a special Christmas this year,' Lucas said finally, his brow furrowing tight. Not really the expression someone should wear when announcing they wanted to spread cheer and joy for Christmas.

'Like I said, I'm completely happy to be your Christmas elf.'

Lucas shot her a sharp glance, slowing his pace as if he was genuinely absorbing her offer. To her surprise, he pointed towards the village below them. 'They're turning the Christmas lights on down at the harbour tonight. Harry's never experienced anything like that, and you're new here in Carey Cove... You wouldn't, by any chance, possibly—'

'Yes,' Kiara interjected, hoping she was putting him out of his misery. 'I would love to go.'

He looked horrified.

Oh, no. She hadn't put him *out* of his misery—she'd thrown him straight into a pit of despair. She was clearly meant to have said no.

She tried to backtrack. 'I mean... I'll go as a friend. Because I'm friendly. But not overly friendly. I don't even have to stand with you, if you don't want. Like a date would. Because it wouldn't be a date.'

Lucas was now looking both horrified and confused.

She soldiered on. 'Unless you mean would I go as Harry's friend? In which case I'm totally on board with— I'll stop there. This talking thing always gets me into trouble at moments like this.' She laughed nervously. 'A *date*!' She feigned disbelief that the word had even been on the table. 'We wouldn't want to start any undue gossip at Carey House, now, would we?' Again, she popped her hands over her mouth, then muttered, 'Please stop talking…please stop talking.'

He looked at her, seriously for a moment, as if actually considering her question, then nodded. 'Good. Grand. Harry will love that. Right!'

He clapped his hands together, as if to bring an end to all the awkwardness, and to the clear relief of both of them they arrived at Carey House, where a shift-change meant there was enough hustle and bustle for her to wave him a quick goodbye and pretend she hadn't just humiliated herself as much as she thought she had.

Lucas closed the door to his surgery and silently banged his head against the wall—one, two, three times—before leaving it there as a low moan escaped his throat.

She didn't think it was a date, did she?

Did he?

No. He wasn't a dater. Not now, anyway. Not even when their chemistry was—

Hang on. Did he *want* it to be a date?

No. Absolutely not. She was a colleague. He was a widower. He had a son to look after.

He thought of the way his body had responded when their hands had inadvertently brushed as they'd both reached to pull shut the small gate at the childminder's. It had been an electric connection. Through *gloves*. Well… In her case mittens. Bright red things, with tiny white reindeer and Christmas trees knitted into the pattern. Not that he'd been staring at her hand and wondering what it would be like to reach out and weave his fingers through hers.

Another low moan emptied out of his chest.

His wife had been right. He was horrendous with women. Terrible at asking them out. Making them feel at ease. In fact, if memory served, he was fairly certain it was Lily who had asked *him* out first back in time. Not that he'd meant to ask Kiara out. This was for Harry. For Christmas. For Harry and Christmas.

He rubbed his hands over his face and shook his head.

The fact he'd managed to woo and win his wife's hand in marriage was a miracle. One miracle in a lifetime was more than enough. Unless you counted Harry, and then that gave him two. Falling in love again was one miracle too many to wish for.

Right?

'Let yourself love again. Don't be afraid to let someone else into your and Harry's lives. And remember to give her flowers.'

His wife's words came to him unbidden. A reminder that he was in charge of his heart. He'd barely registered them at the time. She'd been so very ill, and devoting himself to anything other than their infant son and her care had seemed an impossibility. He'd felt so helpless. So lost. Umpteen years of medical training hadn't prepared him to endure witnessing the woman he'd begun a family with waste away to nothing. So how on earth could he absorb dating advice from that same woman? It had seemed impossible at the time.

So he'd done what he'd imagined any grieving husband might. Closed down the option of ever loving again. And yet here he was, almost three years after losing her, remembering her wish that he and Harry would find room in their hearts for someone else.

Was Kiara that someone?

Eight hours later, as he pulled on his coat and walked to the new mothers' ward, he was still asking himself the same question. Usually a full roster of patients enabled him to push uncomfortable thoughts out of his mind—but not today. Then again, he didn't usually have a date—*not* a date!—waiting for him at the end of the day.

He popped his head into Marnie's room, pleased to see the tell-tale glow of motherhood lighting up the room as Marnie took her daughter into her arms for a feed. Not wanting to interfere with this private moment, he left them to it and headed to the central desk, where he saw Kiara doing a handover with Nya and another midwife—Sophie French. All three of them were wearing multicoloured reindeer antlers. Kiara's were flashing. She leant in and said something in a low voice to the women and they all gave a knowing laugh.

In-jokes already? Only two days on the job and she seemed completely at ease. The fact that she was a good midwife was not in doubt. It was more… Her aura embodied something less tangible. There was a heightened sense of presence about her behaviour that spoke of a feeling of gratitude. He didn't know why, but he got the impression she needed a place like this. Not just Carey House, but Carey Cove.

When he'd moved here with Harry he had been feeling lost, overwhelmed, bereaved. Then he'd driven in along the coastline, seen the beautiful village laid out in lanes that worked their way up the hillside to where, on top, was the golden stone former manor house that was now the cottage hospital. He'd instantly felt as though he'd entered a place of solace. Warmth. Not necessarily a place to forget his past, but a place to heal and then, one day, move forward.

The second Kiara laid eyes on him her expression changed from smiling and bright to purposeful. For reasons he couldn't pinpoint, the shift in mood put him at ease. It was as if she'd read and processed this morning's gaffe over the date/not date invitation and repurposed their outing into what he had intended it to be: for his son.

She shared a quick look with the other women and he didn't miss the mischievous expression Nya sent his way when Kiara disappeared into the midwives' lounge to get her things. He was guessing her humour-filled smile was largely fuelled by his out-of-character slide down the banister yesterday.

'I'm guessing both you and Harry will be hungry,' Kiara said through the muffle of her thrice-wrapped scarf as they left Carey House and headed towards the childminder's. 'If you like, I can meet you down at the Harbour at six. That's when the lights are going on, apparently.'

Her smile was soft and warm. There was no expectation in it and for that he was grateful.

'He's usually had some sort of afternoon snack at the childminder's that tides him over. It's the days at nursery when he needs immediate feeding. I can assure you…a hungry Harry is not a beautiful sight to behold.' He pulled a monster face as evidence.

Kiara put on a shocked expression. 'What? A three-year-old not being beautifully behaved at all times? I refuse to believe it.'

They shared a companionable laugh and carried on walking, the question of when and where to meet still unresolved.

It struck him that she was leaving it up to him. Not in a helpless way. More in the kind of way that meant she wasn't going to push for something that wasn't there. Had her heart been broken, too? Surely not in the way his had. But he sensed a vulnerability in her…a spirited type. One that wasn't going to allow anyone to take command of her heart and treat it without due care.

'Maybe…' he began, just as she started to say something.

A ridiculous politeness pile-on ensued.

'You go…'

'No, you go…'

'Really…'

'Please…'

'You first. I insist.'

Eventually they got to the point where they both stopped talking—although, if he wasn't mistaken, Kiara had succumbed to a case of the giggles behind that extra-long scarf of hers.

Crikey. He was making a right hash of this. He steeled himself and asked the question that had been poised on the tip of his tongue. 'Would you like to join us for supper? Nothing fancy. Or homemade.' He grimaced apologetically. His cooking still had plenty of room for improvement. 'We could have fish and chips down by the harbour?'

Kiara shot him a look, clearly trying to ascertain if she needed to read anything into the invitation. He smiled and held out his hands, as if that was an indicator that he really meant it.

He must have made a convincing show because her smile brightened. 'I do love a hot packet of fish and chips all wrapped up in paper.'

Lucas's smile matched hers in enthusiasm. 'It's great, isn't it? Shame it's not newspaper any more. Sometimes the traditional way of doing things is the best.'

Her smile faltered, then regained purchase so quickly he wouldn't have noticed it if he hadn't been looking. 'Right. That's settled, then. Fish and chips down by the harbour followed by some festive lights.'

She let out a whistle. 'Look at you, getting into the Christmas spirit.'

'It helps having you guide me on the way,' he said, pointing at her antlers. 'Both literally and figuratively.' And he meant it, too.

They collected Harry, who had made and decorated not one, but several gingerbread biscuits. He was instantly bewitched with the blinking antlers. Without a moment's hesitation Kiara switched them from her head to his, sending an *Is this all right?* glance back at Lucas as she did so.

Of course it was. And it also made him want to kick himself. It was magical flourishes like this that his little boy was missing out on by having *him* as his only parent.

After stopping to admire Kiara's dazzling display of Christmas delights, they dropped the biscuits and Harry's backpack off at his house—which Lucas suddenly felt a bit ashamed of. Not because of the house itself. It was a beautiful stone cottage, in keeping with the rest of the village's solid but welcoming aesthetic. It was because it was entirely bereft of Christmas decor. When Harry asked why their house wasn't more like Kiara's, he muttered some excuse about things being lost in the post, but it was, of course, a fiction. The simple truth was that he didn't know how to celebrate Christmas any more.

Kiara didn't comment on it, but he could see that she'd clocked the absence of decorative Christmas cheer and his awkward way of explaining it away.

No wonder his little boy adored her. She embodied the spirit of the season. Warm, generous, kind.

Beautiful.

The thought pulled him up short. She didn't look a thing like Lily—which, if he were psychoanalysing himself, made his attraction to Kiara feel less like a betrayal and more a biological reality.

He buried his head in his hands, grateful that Kiara and Harry were walking ahead of him.

What a Casanova!

If, by some extraordinary turn of events, whatever was happening with Kiara evolved into something romantic, he would have to find a way to express his admiration for her with better word-choices. 'Biological reality' wasn't really a turn of phrase that made a woman swoon. Besides, his response to her was more than biological. It was… It was that same ethereal thing that drew any two strangers together. Kismet? The stars? The spirit of Christmas? He didn't know. All he knew was that it was too strong to ignore. For Harry's sake, obviously. Kiara was the key to making this Christmas a truly memorable one for his little boy.

To his relief, Kiara and Harry commandeered the evening and, mittened hand in mittened hand, led the way down to the harbour, where there was already a small crowd gathering, many with fish and chips.

'Guess we aren't as original as we thought,' Lucas said as they joined the queue.

Kiara's mood only seemed further delighted by his observation. 'It's wonderful being part of something bigger than yourself, isn't it?'

He looked around the harbour area and suddenly saw it through her eyes. She was a stranger here, and yet the atmosphere was anything but exclusive. As people milled in the cobblestoned square, he saw a sea of smiles lifted by a soundscape of laughter and excited chatter. It was a happy place, made cheerier with each new arrival.

One of the retired sailors who was often seen propping up the bar in the local pub was roasting chestnuts in a large metal drum on the harbour's edge. The publicans had set up a stall outside The Dolphin Inn—aka The Dolph—for mulled wine, and from the looks of the number of families in the queue something for the little ones as well. Cornish apple juice with a bit of cinnamon, he guessed from the waft of aroma coming his way.

'You know, you're right.' He smiled down at her as he drew his son in for a hug. 'It feels infectious. In a good way,' he hastily tacked on.

She laughed. 'I would hate the Christmas spirit to be infectious in a bad way.'

She threw him a look that was equal measures delight and caution. 'I meant what I said this morning. I'm happy to help.' She lowered her voice so Harry wouldn't hear. 'If you want me to take Harry to anything that's not appealing to you...' She rattled off a list of events happening around the area, including a Christmas train ride, a nearby Christmas fair and a Christmas-decoration-making afternoon at the weekend.

Lucas laughed. 'You really do love Christmas, don't you?'

She smiled brightly, but her voice was serious and her dark eyes shadowed when she said, 'I love being able to celebrate it as wildly and with as much joy as I want.'

There was a story there. One she clearly felt happy to allude to, but not offer specifics on. He got it. He had his story, too. Moving here hadn't just been about getting out of the house where he'd nursed his wife through to her final moments. It had been about being able to go to the village shop and not have people stare at The Widower. Or having all his patients offer their condolences when he was the one who was meant to be caring for them. He knew, as well, that his son had to be allowed to be Harry Wilde, the energetic little blond boy with curls and a smile to soften even the steeliest of hearts. Not Harry Wilde, the poor little boy who'd lost his mum when he was only a baby. It was a fact. Yes. Just as it was a fact that Lucas was a widower. But he had known they couldn't continue having their loss be the defining factor of who they were and who they might one day become.

'These are amazing!' Kiara beamed when they'd finally got to the front of the queue and were each holding warm bundles of freshly fried fish and deliciously moreish chips doused in salt and vinegar. 'Harry…' Kiara dropped Lucas a complicit wink. 'If you hold on to my hand, I bet I can take you to the best spot to watch the Christmas lights being turned on.'

Harry looked from Kiara to his father, then back again. 'Can we?' he asked his father.

'By all means,' Lucas said, bewildered as to how Kiara managed, after little more than a fortnight in the village, to know already the best place to sit—especially with just about the entire population of Carey Cove being present.

She led them out to the small stone quay where a smattering of sailing and fishing boats were moored. After a quick word with a young man sitting on the back of a mid-sized fishing trawler that was alight with multicoloured lights spanning across its rigging, she stood back, pointed up to the Navigation Bridge, which was strewn with unlit fairy lights, and with a swirl of her free hand announced, 'Ta-da! Your viewing platform, gentlemen.'

Harry looked wide-eyed with disbelief. Lucas realised he probably did, too. 'How on earth—'

She explained as they climbed aboard. 'The captain's wife had a baby yesterday.'

'And you delivered it?' Lucas finished.

She smiled and nodded. 'Her regular midwife had been held up with a more problematic birth, and she kindly agreed to let me step in and help.'

'And somehow, in between teaching her breathing techniques and delivering the baby, you managed to find out that her husband had the best spot to see the Christmas lights.'

She smiled up at him, and yet again Lucas felt that warm glow of connection light up his chest—one that went beyond the parameters of friendship.

'I call it The Distraction Technique,' she quipped, then added, 'She said her husband had decorated the boat specially for her. However, the one scent she hadn't been able to stomach ever since falling pregnant was...'

She looked down at what remained of her meal and then grinned at him.

'Fish?' Lucas finished for her, popping the last piece of his battered cod into his mouth with a smile. 'Well, lucky us.'

'Yes...'

Kiara's smile softened and then, as a light flush caught the apples of her cheeks, she looked back to the village just as a swell of music filled the air. A hush spread across the crowd all the way out to where Lucas, his son and Kiara were perched in the trawler. Lucas hoisted Harry up on to the captain's bench so that he could see the magic of the lights as they came on in their full festive glory.

His fingers twitched with an instinct to take her mittened hand in his. As if sensing the impulse, she glanced over at him and then, clearly feeling the same reticence he was, looked back to the lights, glittering away with nothing but promises of the season yet to come.

CHAPTER FIVE

'HERE YOU ARE, Bethany.' Kiara lifted one tiny swaddled bundle and handed it to the new mum, then once she was settled asked, 'Are you ready for your second son?'

Bethany threw her an anxious smile, tears suddenly blooming in her eyes. 'I guess…' She gave a watery laugh. 'I think I might be missing Graham.'

Kiara smiled warmly and said, 'It's perfectly normal to feel overwhelmed. It's such a shame this is his busy season, but the way your phone keeps pinging to check on you is proof that he wishes he was here instead. And remember…' she tapped the side of her nose '…you can blame hormones for all sorts of things for a while yet.' She handed her a tissue.

Bethany laughed and wiped at her eyes, then held her free arm out to accept her son's twin brother. 'I suppose I'm going to have to get used holding both of them with Graham at work so much.'

'It has only been a day,' Kiara said gently. 'There's no need to be hard on yourself. Motherhood is one of the steepest learning curves there is.'

Kiara caught Bethany's quick glance at her bare ring finger and felt the absence of the natural follow-up question: *Do you have little ones yourself?*

The question had never stung before, when it had felt like such a future certainty. But for the last year it hadn't felt certain—and, although she never begrudged new mums their children, she was beginning to feel the sting of being a singleton.

Kiara stayed close until she was certain Bethany had good purchase on both of her children and then pulled two tiny little elf hats out of her pocket. 'Ready?'

In a sudden about-face, Bethany giggled. 'This is so silly. I mean, they're not even going to remember their first Christmas.'

'But you are! And so is your husband. They're memories for you to share with the boys as they get older.' A thought pricked and lodged in her mind. She had no idea what had happened in Lucas's past, but she was curious as to why Lucas was trying to make Christmas so special for his son but not for himself. Was the fact he hadn't had a spouse or a partner to share his son's earlier Christmases what made it so difficult?

She knew why *she* was marching all guns blazing into the Christmas season. Her ex hadn't just been a married liar. He had been a bit of a control freak—and a snob too. Apparently highly successful surgeons didn't drink cranberry-flavoured cocktails with glittery salt round the edges of the glass, or dance around Christmas trees in Covent Garden for the sheer joy of it.

'Is this okay?' Bethany asked, slipping her own elf hat over her head at a rakish angle.

'Perfect!' Kiara beamed, grateful for the reminder that her life was here in Carey Cove now.

She took a few shots, all at different angles, then, just as she was popping the phone on Bethany's bedside table, heard a soft knock on the doorframe.

Lucas.

Her insides went warm and sparkly.

'Those will be nice additions to the family album,' Lucas said.

Bethany beamed. 'You think?'

'Absolutely.' He indicated the twins, who Kiara was now gently easing back into their shared bassinet. 'It's a nice starter pack of elves you have there.'

Against the odds, Bethany's smile grew even brighter. Kiara gathered up her tablet and a couple of other items and wished Bethany a good night, along with giving her a reminder that her husband would be calling in for a visit in an hour's time.

'Nice day?' asked Lucas.

'Very.' Kiara beamed. 'We have a dozen new November babies and it's only a few days into the month!' She laughed and gave him a wink that halfway through took on a flirtatious flare she'd never known she possessed. 'Valentine's Day has got a lot to answer for.'

Lucas smiled, then slowed his pace. 'Speaking of Valentine's...'

Kiara's eyes shot to his. Was he going to ask her out for next February? That was forward planning on a whole new level. However, they did say good things came to those who waited, so...

Lucas must have seen the confused look in her eyes, because he pulled a face of his own and rubbed his hand along his jaw—clean-shaven again today—and then dropped it. 'That was a terrible segue. I wasn't meaning to talk about Valentine's at all.'

Her heart surprised her by plummeting. Of course he wasn't. She was stupid to have even gone there in her mind. Stupid winking…turning everything ridiculously flirty. She made a silent vow never to wink again.

He paused, and then clawed one of his hands through his hair as he started and stopped talking a couple of more times.

Kiara gave him a sidelong look. 'I'm not so scary that you can't just ask me something outright, am I?'

'No, I—'

Kiara bit down on her lip as her heart skipped a beat. He was going to ask her out on another date/not a date!

'I was wondering if—'

'Yes!' she blurted. 'I mean…if it's more Christmas stuff with Harry, I'm in. Like I said the other day… I'm your Ghost of Christmas Present.'

The instant she said the words she regretted them. There was very clearly a Ghost of Christmas Past in Lucas's life…just as there was in hers…only his seemed more ingrained in him.

'I mean… Sorry… I…' She pulled a face, then said, 'Should we start this whole conversation again? My mum calls them do-over moments.'

Lucas's lips twitched into a grateful smile. 'Your mother sounds like a very wise woman.'

To Kiara's delight, his eyes grew bright as he lifted his eyebrows and cupped his chin with his hand, a finger tapping away on his cheek, as if he was in thoughtful consideration of how one commenced a 'do-over', then abruptly turned and walked away.

'Hey!' she called after him. 'Where are you going?'

Quick as a flash, he whirled around and with a warm, confident smile said, 'Oh, hi, Kiara. I'm glad I caught you here. Harry and I were thinking of heading over to the Christmas market and fair a bit further down the coast tonight. We were wondering if you'd care to join us.'

Happiness bubbled from Kiara's toes all the way up to the sparkly Santa hat she was wearing. She felt as if Lucas had dropped a bath bomb in her insides. 'Excellent do-over,' she said, impressed.

'You think?' He doffed an invisible cap. 'I aim to please.'

Their eyes caught and held. For a precious moment Kiara felt linked to him in a way she hadn't imagined ever feeling with a man again. Not after last year. The energy between them had built into something almost tangible. A magnetic force connecting them in a way that surely had to make their trip to a Christmas market and fair more date-like than not.

And then Nya appeared.

'Hello, you two.' She looked much more amused than bemused as she asked, 'May I ask if you plan to hold your little staring contest here in the corridor for the foreseeable future? Or is it just a temporary thing?'

Kiara, who heard the teasing tone in her voice, turned to her and pointedly blinked her eyes. 'That's us done.'

'We're heading off to the Christmas fair just outside Mousehole,' Lucas said. 'For Harry.'

'Yes,' Kiara pounced on the much less date-sounding description. 'Harry does love his Christmas bling.'

Nya gave an approving nod, then shooed them out of the corridor towards the stairs, her voice taking on the tone of a concerned mother. 'Two nights out in the same week? That little boy's going to be over the moon. You'd best get a move on. Here's your coat, Kiara. Lucas, make sure you wear a hat. Set a good example for your son. On you go, now, and make sure you get Harry home early. It's a school night!'

When Nya had finally headed back to her desk, Kiara and Lucas shared a giggle. 'Well, that's us told, then,' said Kiara.

They laughed again, and expressed their mutual admiration for Nya. Kiara felt no compunction about enthusing about her being a good boss. The best she'd had, actually. Warm, but exacting. Generous and humane. It made working here really feel like being part of team rather than the cog in a huge machine that she'd sometimes felt like back in London.

Exchanging information about their days at work, they briskly made their way down the hill, collected Harry and, at Kiara's suggestion, enjoyed some cheese on toast at her house, with the added bonus of Harry being allowed to help Kiara select which box of decorations to put out next. Then they set off down the road towards Mousehole.

Before they'd even rounded the corner to the next cove they could see the lights. Harry, who seemed to be filled with jumping beans tonight, was clapping his hands in anticipation.

When they got out of the car they walked to the central green, where the Christmas market was being held, they all held their breath as one.

In the very centre of the square were three enormous ice sculptures—a snowman, a reindeer and, tallest of all, a huge, jolly Santa Claus with an enormous bag of presents slung over his shoulder. Kiara had no idea how they'd done it, but frozen into the 'bag' were actual toys. A nutcracker, a teddy bear, a doll, and a dozen or so other old-fashioned toys that made the visual display all the more remarkable. The sculptures were illuminated, so that they sparkled like diamonds.

Harry's eyes were so wide, Kiara could actually see the sculptures reflected in them. She knelt down so that she was at eye level with Harry. 'Which one's your favourite?

'The reindeer,' he said after a moment's hesitation. And then, 'The snowman.' He threw her a panicked look. 'Can't I love all of them just the same?'

'Of course you can!' Kiara laughed pulling him in for a cosy hug. 'You've got a huge heart, haven't you, Harry? Such a big, huge heart.'

She let herself fall into the moment. Enjoy the little boy arms around her neck. His energy. His scent. A little boy elixir made up of crisp cheese, earth and soap. She looked up and realised Lucas was watching the pair of them with an intensity the moment didn't necessarily warrant. But…who knew? Maybe it did.

A memory of her reaction to seeing Lucas that very first time he'd loomed above her sprang to mind. It had been visceral, her response to him. Core-deep. As if somehow she'd been waiting to meet him for her entire life.

She felt a shift then. Something in her gave way. Something that hadn't managed to move since her relationship had come to such an explosive end. It felt as if light was pouring into the little cracks and crevices inside her. Fissures she'd thought she'd blocked, so that she wouldn't ever allow herself to feel so hurt again. But this feeling was different. There was a vulnerability to it, yes. But there was also hope and possibility infused with the warmth that she knew came from meeting Lucas.

He held out a hand and helped her to stand up, and although they didn't continue to hold hands as they walked around the fair, with Harry running from stall to stall, intent on sampling all the Christmas treats, she still felt the strength of his hand as it had wrapped round hers for those few seconds. And something deep inside her told her she would miss that touch for evermore.

'You all set, mate?'

Harry wobbled uncertainly in Lucas's hands for a moment, and then, when one of the teenaged girls hired as a coach for the special pre-schoolers' skate session held out both of hers for Harry to join the rest of the little ones on the ice, Harry took them without so much as a backward glance.

Despite the hit of loss, Lucas had to smile. His son's first moment on skates…

'It's amazing how they take to it, isn't it?' Kiara appeared beside him, holding two steaming mugs. 'Hot chocolate to keep you warm?'

He took the mug gratefully. 'They've really done this whole event up to the nines, haven't they?'

It was truly magical. But rather than agree, Kiara let out a contented sigh and took a big sip of her hot chocolate, which left an impressive dollop of whipped cream on her nose.

'Here. You've got some…' He dug into his pocket and pulled out a clean handkerchief. Their eyes locked as he held it just above her nose, poised for action, and asked mischievously, 'Unless you were keeping it for later?'

'Hmm…' she began, as if considering the option. 'I do like a bit of whipped cream before bed, but…' Her tongue swept across her bottom lip just before her upper teeth caught it tight. Her cheeks pinkened, as if she'd admitted something slightly too intimate for the occasion.

He took a step back and offered her the handkerchief instead of wiping the cream off himself, as he had planned to, suddenly aware of how many of their interchanges bore the hue of flirtation about them. Interchanges neither of them had pushed beyond a glance or a flush of acknowledgement.

He felt an abrupt and urgent need to explain where he was in life. How meeting her had opened up a rush of feelings and…yes… he'd admit it…an attraction he hadn't thought he'd ever experience again.

Before he could stop himself, he said, 'Harry's mother would've loved to see a moment like this.'

He nodded out to the ice rink, where Harry was now holding hands with a little girl, her hair in near identical blonde curls to his peeking out from underneath a knitted cap with snowflakes woven into the design. The two of them looked like a Christmas card.

He tried to say more, but the words caught in his throat. Because if his wife had lived, he wouldn't be here with Kiara—he'd be here watching Harry, and one of them would most likely have a baby strapped to their chest. Perhaps a little girl. Or another boy. It wouldn't matter. They'd said they wanted children, not boys or girls. Because it hadn't mattered if they'd be picking up mud-splattered jeans or tutus. What had mattered was family. Having babies, then toddlers, then school kids, then teens, to nurture and love until one day they had children of their own. He'd seen it all so clearly back then, but now the future…it was a blank slate. One that, courtesy of a Christmas-mad midwife who'd just happened to move to the same tiny village in the same nook of Cornwall as he had, was now bathed in possibility.

He looked into Kiara's eyes and saw nothing but compassion there. And a thousand questions he realised he was going to have to answer.

'She passed away,' he said simply. 'Cancer,' he added by means of explanation. It had been one that had crept up on them a matter of weeks after they'd found out Lily was pregnant. The malignant cells had attacked and reformed into tumours with such ferocity it had completely blindsided them. 'Gestational trophoblastic disease.'

Kiara gasped. It was clear from the expression on her face—and the fact she was a midwife, so probably had encountered similar cases—that there was no need to explain about this particular, quite rare form of cancer.

He gave a few details. The discovery of the cancer. His wife's refusal to have chemotherapy, terrified that the treatment had the potential to compromise their son's welfare. Their disagreement. Their ultimate compromise... She would get treatment as soon as Harry was born. And then, to their horror, the realisation it was far too late.

Lucas knew that his normal voice had been replaced by the strange, automated version of it that had come to him in the days and weeks following the funeral, but he wasn't sure what would happen if he allowed even an ounce of the emotion he was feeling to sneak to the surface.

A little voice rose loud and clear in his subconscious. *You'll bend or break, Lucas. And I know which way I think you'll go.*

His wife had believed he had the power to

bend and bounce back. He'd tearfully told her she had more faith in him than he had in himself. That there would be no regrouping from a loss like the one he and Harry were about to endure. The day she'd died he'd felt as if his entire body had been filled with darkness. It would have consumed him if he hadn't had his son. This tiny creature, only a few months old, wholly dependent upon him.

Throughout his explanation Kiara stood solidly, her eyes glued to him as he spoke, her attention unwavering, her hot chocolate untouched. He knew she was there for him. One hundred percent. And, as if her strength of character was physically supporting him, for the first time since he'd lost his wife he spoke freely about what he'd gone through.

He hadn't bounced back. He'd felt as if he'd been cleft in two…one half of him with his wife and the life they were meant to have led, and the other half desperately trying to gain purchase on the life Harry deserved to be living. One in the here and now.

'Truth be told,' he said to Kiara, 'I just never imagined doing anything but breaking into a thousand pieces if a scenario like this one ever arose.'

'What do you mean?' Her brow furrowed in confusion.

'I—' he began, and then backtracked. 'Being out with a woman,' he said. Then, when her response was one difficult-to-read blink, he added, 'You know… Not on a date, but in a situation where people who didn't know we weren't on a date might think we were together.'

'Oh…' Kiara's voice drew the sound out as if the thought had never occurred to her. She let her gaze drift out to the rink, where Harry was, once again, picking himself up off the ice.

Her reaction threw him. It *was* mutual, wasn't it? The attraction they shared? And, to be honest, to him this felt like a date.

A swift, icy-cold spear of panic lanced through him. Had he read this situation entirely incorrectly? Had she genuinely meant that she wanted to give Harry the best Christmas ever and that was where it ended? Perhaps he was the one desperate for a connection and had been dotting 'i's and crossing 't's where there hadn't been any.

Or maybe…

He looked at her. Really looked at her. And saw what he hadn't before. A desire to listen and be there for him but a wariness not to overstep. A nervousness about crossing that line.

To be fair, it was a big ask. To pour his heart out about losing the love of his life to someone with whom he shared a physical and increasingly emotional attraction and expect her to say, *Oh, that's sad...do you want to kiss me?*

Not that Kiara would ever do anything as crass as that, and not that he was even close to ready to be stripping off and jumping in the hay with her except in his dreams, but he'd dreamt a very erotic dream about her. And each time they'd met he'd felt a magnetic energy shift between them on more than one occasion. Including tonight, when he'd pulled her up to stand and been so tempted to keep her mittened hand in his.

And now he was throwing a bucket of ice on what should, by all counts, be a romantic evening.

Was he self-sabotaging?

Or testing himself?

He hadn't cracked into a million tiny shards of glass. Or lost himself in a sea of misery and grief. He hadn't run. Or broken down. Or lashed out at the world around him for the cruelty that was cancer.

Quite the opposite. He was standing in front of a woman he shared an undeniable attraction with. His feet were solidly on the ground. He was, to his astonishment, offering Kiara what he hoped was a smile. It was the least and the most he could offer her at this moment. And he hoped to heaven she could see that.

When she returned his cautious smile, his heart bloomed and began pounding out large, approving thumps against his ribcage.

Maybe he was doing it right. Maybe, after a loss like his, you just took it step by step. One sip of hot chocolate after the next. One walk home under a starry sky with her mittened hand tucked in his.

One first kiss?

He almost stumbled back a step at the thought, then forced himself to regroup. Life was precious. He of all people should know that. It wouldn't just be stupid to crumble at this, the first and probably most important hurdle of his friendship with Kiara. It would be a form of self-sabotage that would serve no purpose.

If he was being truly honest with himself, he knew Lily would've liked her. They weren't peas in a pod. Not by a long shot. But Kiara championed everything he valued and was everything he had sought in a woman when he'd been a young singleton back in med school. Honest. Kind. Infused with strong family values.

Kiara brought a smile to his lips more often than not. His son thought she was on another level. She was incredible at her job. She'd brought more Christmas cheer to her home than he'd seen anywhere in a lifetime of celebrating Christmas.

'And that,' he said, with a weird half-bow he hoped would break the awkwardness of his confession, 'is our origin story. What brought us here to Carey Cove, anyway.'

Kiara pressed her free hand to her mouth, her red-mittened fingers pushing the colour out of her lips. Her cheeks, so recently flushed with pleasure, were now pale. 'I'm so sorry, Lucas. I didn't know.'

He shook his head. 'You're possibly the only one in a ten-mile radius who doesn't.'

'Did you want it to be a secret?'

Her question was a genuine one.

'No,' he answered truthfully. 'It was more that we put ourselves on a path that led forward, you know?'

Kiara shook her head. Unsurprisingly, she was clearly unable to understand his feeble attempt to explain what he'd wanted from the move. He realised this was actually the first time he'd tried to put it into words. He took a sip of his hot chocolate and gave her a smile before refocusing his gaze on his son—the reason behind the move.

'Everyone knew Lily where we were. I guess, rather than having Harry live in the shadow of someone he was never going to meet, I wanted him to live in the light. I thought moving would help us both focus on what we did have. Not on what we didn't.'

He tried to keep his tone light, but it was impossible to keep the rough edges of emotion at bay.

'You two sound as if you were very much in love.'

Tears glistened in Kiara's eyes, and it surprised him to realise his instinct was to dab them away for her. To care for her. And not just as a friend. He wanted something more. He simply didn't know how to make that shift.

He nodded. 'Yes. We were.'

He took the handkerchief which Kiara had balled up in her hand and folded it into a neat triangle with the bit of whipped cream tucked on the inside. He handed it back to her and pointed to her eyes.

'I suppose the main thing I have is that I've known true happiness. So should it ever cross my path again...'

He left the sentence hanging, but when the atmosphere between them threatened to shift into something that felt more intimate than any other silence they'd shared, Kiara asked, 'Did Harry…? I mean, how has he dealt with things?'

Lucas shook his head and gave his jaw a rub. 'He was only a few months old when Lily died, so he doesn't have any memories of her apart from what I've told him.'

His eyes scanned the rink until he found Harry who, in a moment of bravery, had broken away from the chain of youngsters only to end up falling on his bum.

Lucas gave a little laugh. 'That's roughly what it's been like for the pair of us. Falling down. Getting up. Falling down again. Finding a new way to get up. Well…' He shot her a self-effacing smile. 'That's mostly been me. Harry grabs on to all of the happy things in life and runs with them. I'm still learning from him, to be honest.'

'I can't even imagine…'

He could tell from the depth of emotion in her voice that she was feeling his pain as if it was her own. 'Thank you,' he said, meaning it. 'I dare say there are a few things I could learn from you, too.'

Their eyes caught and held. He felt as if he

could see straight into her heart then. And what he saw was pure and kind.

'Has moving here helped?' Kiara asked, and her question was weighted with something else. Something personal.

'Yes,' he answered simply, hoping his straightforward answer would help with her unasked question.

Will it help me, too?

'The people at Carey Cove are so kind,' he continued, returning his gaze to his son. 'And, of course, so are the folk up at the cottage hospital. I only worked in one GP surgery before—before we lost Lily—and I feel like I've really landed on my feet here.'

'I'm so glad. I can't even imagine… Especially with Harry being so young.' She made a quick correction. 'I can't imagine going through what you have at any phase of life. Losing someone you clearly loved so very much. I'm guessing that might be why you find celebrations hard? Christmas, anyway…' She gave an awkward laugh. 'Seeing as it's the only time of celebration I've known you.'

He was gripped with an unexpectedly intense desire not only to see Christmas through her eyes, but all celebrations. New Year's Eve, Easter, Valentine's Day…

That last one caught him up short. Was he really feeling this? Attraction and interest in a woman to whom he was explaining about his deceased wife?

'Don't be afraid to let someone else into yours and Harry's lives. And remember to give her flowers.'

Lucas stared at his son for a few concentrated moments, allowing himself to absorb just how easily his son had taken to Kiara in their handful of outings. He leant in close, letting their shoulders brush against one another's, and said, 'Thank you for showing me how special it can be.'

'Pleasure,' she whispered back.

It's all mine, he thought.

Acting on an impulse, he put his arm around her shoulders and pulled her close to him for a hug as they both watched Harry fall once again and then, with an ear-to-ear grin, get back up again and wave to the pair of them as if he'd been doing it all his life.

CHAPTER SIX

'ARE YOU SURE this is all right?' Kiara winced, not wanting to overstep. She held out the flyers so Hazel could take a proper look. Not that they were hard to read even from a distance. She'd made them bright and cheery—Christmas colours, of course—and the font was extra-large.

Mince Pies at Mistletoe Cottage!

She realised it was short notice, but last night, when she hadn't been able to sleep and had been decorating inside her home, she'd decided a mini gala in the form of mulled wine, mince pies and, of course, a huge swag of mistletoe would give the fund she'd been accruing for First Steps an added boost.

'Of course, love.' Hazel dug around in the reception desk drawer for a moment, obviously looking for a couple of drawing pins so that Kiara could put her flyers up on the noticeboard. 'Who doesn't love a mini gala?' Then she gave Kiara a slightly confused look. 'Although, come to think of it, I don't think I know what a mini gala is, so I'll have to go just to satisfy my curiosity. Ah! Here we are.'

Kiara beamed as Hazel handed across a small clear plastic box of pins. They were tiny little Christmas trees! 'Aw... Thank you. And you do know it's for charity? This definitely isn't for personal gain.'

'I do, love, and let me assure you the enjoyment the villagers are getting from your incredible decorations is—well, it's like nothing Carey Cove has ever experienced before. You're a wonder.'

Kiara flushed and, to her embarrassment, felt the opening prickle of a rush of emotion tease the back of her nose. She swallowed it back, but felt it lodge somewhere between her heart and her throat.

Taking the pins, Kiara quickly turned away and, with a fastidiousness the task didn't really warrant, began to display her flyers.

She was just feeling sensitive this morning. Perhaps a bit *too* sensitive after her night out with Lucas and Harry.

It had been lovely, of course, but finding out about Lucas's wife and seeing first-hand how much he'd loved her had stuck a pin in the elation she usually felt whenever their eyes met. She was positive she hadn't been imagining it—that electric connection she felt each time they looked into one another's eyes—but there was no chance she would be able to find herself any room in a heart that was clearly filled to the brim with love for another woman.

And no chance she would even try.

Elbowing out Harry's mother to make room for herself?

Not a chance.

She'd unwittingly already played that game, and had definitely not come out the winner. She'd spent the past year re-inflating her crushed hopes, dreams, ego…you name it. All of them had been smashed beyond all recognition. The woman she'd rebuilt herself into was someone she liked. But no matter how brave a face she put on she was still fragile. And she certainly didn't want to experience heartache like that ever again. So from here on out she'd wear the firmest of emotional armour when she was around Lucas. She'd keep her heart safe…like Rapunzel in her turret.

As if to prove it to herself, she took a hold of her ponytail and twirled it into a very self-contained bun. *There.* No princes would be climbing up her hair. Not tonight. Not ever.

'Mince pies at Mistletoe Cottage, eh? Sounds like a dream evening. Are father and son duos invited?'

Lucas's warm voice wound its way round her spine like molten caramel. She steadied the wobble in her knees and smiled brightly, hoping her face didn't betray how she was really feeling. 'Yes. Everyone's welcome.'

Lucas's smile stayed put, but he frowned at her comment, the creases in his forehead actively registering the statement she was really making: *You're not a special guest.*

'Ooh! Mince pies at Mistletoe Cottage?' Sophie, her fellow midwife, joined them at the noticeboard. 'Is this for everyone?'

'Absolutely! The more the merrier,' chirped Kiara, and then, remembering how cool she'd just been with Lucas added, 'All for charity.'

Cringe!

'Hey, Lucas…' Sophie's bright blue eyes suddenly widened. 'Are you going to see Santa tonight? You and Harry?'

Lucas looked at Kiara first, as if to double-check that he hadn't forgotten any plans they'd made, then shook his head. 'I hadn't heard Santa Claus was coming to town. I'd better watch out!'

'Ha-ha. Very funny.'

Sophie rolled her eyes and Kiara choked on a genuine laugh. The joke was silly, but funny. To her, anyway. She'd always imagined having a boyfriend who told goofy jokes. Dad jokes, really. And that the boyfriend would become her husband and a father one day.

Despite her best efforts to keep the image at bay, a mental list of the ways in which Lucas was absolutely perfect for her unfurled in her mind like a list of Christmas wishes.

'What about you, Kiara? A bunch of us are going to be there. Want to come?'

'Oh, I...' She looked at Lucas. His expression was quizzical, as if he was looking to her for a read on the situation. She didn't blame him for being confused. Yesterday Kiara would have pounced on the invitation and insisted Harry and Lucas join her. How on earth was he to understand why today Kiara was hesitating?

But, as if reading her mind, Lucas said, 'Harry has had quite a few nights out this week. Perhaps a night off—'

'But it's Santa!'

The words were out before Kiara could

stop them. It appeared giving Harry the world's best Christmas experience trumped her own discomfort.

Lucas's smile brightened, the light returning to those grey eyes of his. 'You sure? He might get cranky.'

She pursed her lips. 'Cranky-schmanky. If I can handle women giving birth on a near daily basis, I can handle an overtired little boy. Besides...' she looked to Sophie '...if it's for the little ones, it isn't going to be late, is it?'

Sophie said no, and filled them in on the time and place. A village green about five miles further down the coast. 'So, see you there?' she asked.

'Yes, definitely,' Kiara answered, with a confidence she was trying to get the rest of her body to feel.

Sophie said she was off early, so would meet them there, then went off to the birthing wing where a patient was waiting. Which left Kiara and Lucas standing there on their own.

'You sure you're okay with this?' Lucas asked. 'I don't want to strong-arm you into anything.'

'Yes, of course.' She couldn't let Harry down just because his sexy dad was off-limits. It wasn't fair. And if she'd learnt anything over the past year, it was that happiness came in the smallest of moments. 'I can't wait to see his little face light up when Santa arrives. I wonder how he'll do it. There isn't any snow forecast, so…will he arrive by boat?'

Lucas shrugged, his smile now more relaxed. 'Who knows? We'll all have to wait and see. I'll pick you up after your shift?'

Her resident butterflies lifted and did a few gentle laps of her tummy. 'Sure. Sounds good.' Then, as if to prove to herself he was only a friend, she added, 'See you then, mate.'

If Lucas thought her turn of phrase was peculiar—which it was—he didn't let her see it. Instead, he gave her a little salute and disappeared into the GP surgery.

At which point, she finally let her knees wobble.

It was going to be a long day…and an even longer night.

'Ooh!' Harry was all eyes, and his mouth was a big round O as they took in the scene.

It seemed every village form Carey Cove to Land's End and back again was doing its utmost to celebrate the arrival of Christmas. Even Lucas, who was now happy to admit he'd been Christmas resistant, was feeling a buzz of excitement as more and more children's excited chatter filled the air.

'Daddy. I can't see.'

'Would he like to ride on my shoulders?' Kiara asked, a hint of shyness tinging her voice.

Lucas bent down to pick up his son, hoping to hide his reaction to the walls that seemed to have appeared between them since he'd told Kiara about Lily. He hated it that she felt awkward around him, and wondered if this was what it would be like if he were to proactively go out and start dating.

He checked the thought, and with it felt a new understanding take purchase in his chest. He didn't want to proactively start dating. Downloading apps. Letting the kindly women at the bakery who'd been all but begging him to let them set him up with their daughters organise a few 'chance meetings'.

But he did want to see Kiara. And not as a colleague. Or even as a friend. More as…a possibility.

But he found it impossible to say as much.

'How about we take turns?' he suggested. 'I'll do round one.'

He dipped his head to see if he'd hit the right note and was rewarded with one of those soft smiles of hers. The kind where her teeth skimmed along her bottom lip as if she wasn't going to allow herself a full grin. Feeling as though he was at least heading in the right direction, he popped Harry onto his shoulders so his son could properly ogle the huge throne where Santa would be sitting when he arrived.

Kiara shot him another one of those shy smiles, then shifted her gaze towards the huge tree at the edge of the green, its thick evergreen boughs expertly swirled with festive lights and topped with a sparkling star.

'Have you two got your tree up yet?' she asked.

Lucas's smile turned guilty. 'Not strictly speaking.'

'Are there plans to put one up?'

Again, out of Harry's earshot, he had to confess, 'It's not exactly on my "To Do" list.'

A purposeful look wiped away any shyness she'd been carrying in her features. 'I am afraid I'm going to have to stage an intervention. Three-year-old boys who love Christmas as much as your son does should have a Christmas tree.'

'Oh, no. You've already done so much for—' He stopped himself. 'That would be great. We'd really like that.'

She beamed and gave Harry's foot a tap. 'You all right up there? Not too cold?'

Harry bounced his feet up and down, clapping his hands and singing, 'Happy! Happy!'

Kiara laughed as well, her smile softening into something so pure Lucas felt as though its warmth was physically touching his heart.

He had to admit, Christmas fan or not, he was moved by the way Kiara behaved with his son. Her heart was completely open with him. When Harry laughed about something she joined in completely organically. When he was hurt—as he had been that first day, after their literal run-in—her immediate instinct was to wipe away his tears and bring a smile to his face. To care for him.

The ache in his heart doubled.

He'd never imagined another woman caring for his son as a parent, but here was proof it could be done. With both ease and grace. And perhaps, one day, with love…?

Kiara must've felt his gaze, because she turned to him and said, almost apologetically, 'I'm so grateful that you and Harry are letting me tag along on your Christmas adventures.'

'What?' Her comment was seriously out of left field. 'Not at all! It's us who should be thanking you.'

She scrunched her nose up, clearly unconvinced.

He was about to ask her where all this was coming from, but he thought he knew the answer.

It had come from him.

Even thinking it brought a thousand emotions to the surface. His body felt as if it was being torn in two directions.

This was it. The turning point he'd heard other widowers describe.

The moment when he could choose to devote himself to a familiar but heartbreaking past—or look, at long last, towards a new future.

'You're the one who's making this season special for Harry,' he said. 'For both of us,' he added, a second too late.

She blinked, and her gaze shifted from him to Harry, then back to the hum of human life around them. Families, mostly. He watched an invisible cloak of loneliness wrap around her as she took it all in. Mothers dabbing bits of food off their children's faces or clothes. Fathers doing the same as he was, hoisting their children up onto their shoulders or giving them a piggyback. Older children helping little ones with their mittens or hats.

He knew in that moment that whatever it

was that had happened to her in London had stolen this from her. Being part of a family. And, worse, she'd been made to feel ashamed for wanting it. His heart ached for her. He might not have his wife, but he had his son, and the power of that was incalculable.

Could he offer her a cobbled-together version of a family?

The thought all but knocked him sideways.

He *really* liked her, and it wasn't just as a new friend and colleague. But he was still brand-new to navigating the world as a single dad. His flirting skills were properly rusty— and there was also the fact that he had no idea what he could promise.

Listen to your heart, you idiot! Life's full of risks.

An epiphany struck. Loving Lily had been one of those risks.

Aren't you happy you loved her when you had the chance? If you hadn't, you wouldn't have Harry.

The voice in his head had a point. But on the flipside… His number one responsibility was Harry. What if he got attached to Kiara? Too attached? And what if things didn't work out? Kiara was obviously trying for a fresh start in life and who knew? Maybe Carey

Cove was all well and good for her right now…but would it be always?

Not everything's an 'always'. That doesn't mean it's wise to run away from life. Run to it. You've only got this one chance to be you.

Rather than ignore the voice in his head, Lucas reached out and did what he should have done the other night. What he should be doing right now. He took her hand in his, then gave it a light squeeze. 'I appreciate everything you're doing for me. It's not easy bringing Christmas cheer to a bah-humbugger like me.'

She looked at him, startled, but then, as his words registered, her lips began to twitch with hints of a smile. 'Anyone would be happy to do it,' she countered.

'Rubbish. Harry deserves the best and we got the best.' He saw her smile flicker with pride. 'We wouldn't be having nearly as much fun if you weren't our festive Christmas guide. Would we buddy?'

He looked up at his son, who had been distracted by a loud hum overhead. One that was growing louder by the second.

When he looked back at Kiara, she too was looking up at the sky, but he could feel her fingers lightly pressing into his palm. A calmness came over him. A peace he hadn't expected to feel when he touched another woman in this way.

Suddenly it was as plain as day: Kiara felt the same way about him as he felt about her. There was a shared attraction. But they had both been hurt. Possibly in very different ways. So they'd have to tread carefully. Respectfully.

He returned the gentle squeeze, half tempted to put his arm round her and pull her in close, when all of the sudden a huge searchlight appeared from the ground, illuminating the tell-tale red and white of one of the local Search and Rescue helicopters. The door swung open as the helicopter expertly hovered overhead.

To the crowd's delight, Santa Claus appeared, one foot already stepping onto the guard rail as he hooked himself onto a winch, and then slung an enormous red bag over his shoulder.

'Oh, my *days*! I can't look!'

Lucas and Kiara dropped their linked hands as their colleague Sophie's voice cut into the warm bubble of calm surrounding them. He wasn't sure who had let go of the other first, but it was clear neither of them wanted the rumour mill to include the two of them.

'Everything all right, Sophie?' Kiara put an arm around the other woman's shoulders, the concern in her voice taking the lead.

'No. Seriously…no.' Sophie shaded her eyes and looked down at the ground as the crowd cheered. 'How can they all watch?'

Lucas looked up to see what could be causing her such distress. Santa was being winched down…no surprise there…

'Ooh, I can't look!' Sophie repeated, looking down at the ground and stamping her feet, as if willing herself into another time and place.

'Are you afraid of heights?' Kiara asked, dipping her head so her colleague could see her face.

'Big-time. That Santa's either insane or more intent on spreading good cheer than any other Santa I've ever seen in my life. I mean—' She threw a panicked look at Harry, who had just looked down at her. 'Not that I've met any different Santas. That's Santa. Obviously.' She winced. 'Are you sure you're all right up there, Harry?'

Harry clapped his hands, then pointed up to the sky. 'I want to be up *there*!'

Sophie gave a low moan.

Lucas gave her back a gentle rub. 'You're

looking a bit pale, Sophie. Can we get you something?'

'I can take you somewhere to sit down and get you some water if you like,' Kiara offered, throwing Lucas an *Is that all right?* look.

Of course it was. Anything Sophie needed. Poor woman. He had the opposite situation going on. A three-year-old boy bouncing on his shoulders with sheer delight, begging to climb up and meet Santa.

Kiara put a hand on his arm and in a low voice said, 'I'm going to take Sophie away from the crowd for a bit. If we don't catch up at the end of the event, I'll figure out a way to get back to the village on my own.'

'Don't be silly. We wouldn't leave you here.'

Her eyes snapped to his as if he'd said something much more personal. More intimate. And he wondered again what on earth had happened to her back in London to make her so grateful for simple kindnesses.

But maybe they weren't simple. Perhaps those were the moments that should be cherished the most. Fingers brushing. Eyes locking. Heartbeats pounding out the beats as a reminder that you were alive. After all, those few precious moments when their fingers had been interlocked were still buzzing through his bloodstream like a brand-new life force.

Later, after Santa had handed out small gifts to all the children and heard their wishes, then been winched back up to the helicopter to the cheers of the crowd, Kiara found her way to them. She said she'd walked Sophie to her car in the end and, after ensuring she felt well enough to drive, had left her to go home.

Harry fell asleep almost the instant he was buckled into his car seat, the brand-new teddy bear from Santa clutched in his arms.

They drove home in relative silence, and when they stopped at her house—a beacon of Christmas cheer that now instantly brought a smile to his lips because he knew who was behind it—Lucas decided to tell Kiara just how much having her in their lives meant to him.

Just as he began to stumble through some words, Kiara unbuckled her seatbelt and quietly eased herself out of the car with her finger to her lips. She pointed to Harry with a whispered, 'See you in the morning.'

He waited until she got to her front door, and when she waved goodbye and disappeared behind it an emptiness filled him he hadn't expected to feel.

When he got home, and was tucking Harry into bed after their usual night-time story, Harry curled up to him and asked, 'Can Kiara stay here sometimes? I think she'd be good at telling stories, too.'

The question knocked the air out of him. It was an innocent enough question for a child. His little boy could hardly know about Lucas's very adult dream and nor would he. Harry was simply stating a fact: He liked it when they were all together.

He wasn't trying to replace Lily. To be fair to his son, he didn't even remember her enough to miss her. He'd only ever known life with the two of them, and yet he seemed instinctively to know there was something missing in their lives. One more piece to the puzzle they had yet to complete.

Instead of answering—because he simply didn't know how—Lucas kissed his son's head, wished him sweet dreams and told him to sleep well so they'd be on time to pick Kiara up in the morning.

'But that's hours away!' Harry whined through a yawn. And then, as exhaustion took over, he fell asleep, his new teddy tucked beneath his hand.

A restless sensation took hold of Lucas. He wandered through the house picking things up and putting them down somewhere else, then returning them to their original position. He turned on all the lights. He turned them off. Pulled the curtains shut. Opened the curtains. Rather than seeing the things he had done, he saw all the things he hadn't. There were beds, and sofas, and even a throw cushion or two. But it didn't feel like his childhood home had done, with designated places for all the furniture to be rearranged to make room for the Christmas tree. The presents. The space where he and his siblings would play with their toys for days after, until his mother, fed up with tripping over train tracks or dolls' houses, finally made them take their shiny new possessions up to their rooms.

It didn't feel like a home at all.

And, although he'd managed to pick up the pieces after Lily's death—raise his son, find a new job, find a new house—he still seemed to be missing one elemental part of himself.

The next morning was a disaster. He and Harry had both slept poorly—to the point when Harry had left his own bed and crawled in with Lucas…something he hadn't done for months. Once sleep had finally come, they'd both slept through the alarm.

Getting themselves together had been chaos. And now Harry was overtired and cranky. Irritable to the point where Lucas wondered if he was coming down with something. At least he was with the childminder today and not at nursery. The calm atmosphere there would do him good.

When they reached Kiara's house, Harry dropped his scooter and ran to the door, demanding that Lucas pick him up so he could reach the bell. After several unanswered ding-dongs they were forced to accept that she wasn't at home, and Harry had a proper meltdown.

There were tears. Wailing. Tiny fists pummelling the artificial snow blanket laid out beneath the dancing penguins. If he hadn't been so tired himself, Lucas might've tried to console his son more than he did. Instead, he knelt down in the 'snow' beside him, rubbing his back and saying on a loop, 'I know, son. I know...'

He wished she was here, too.

After he'd finally managed to soothe Harry, he dropped him off at the childminder, who assured him she'd dole out some extra TLC, and possibly an extra nap today. She also suggested a quiet night at home to counterbalance the excitement of the season.

She said it kindly enough, but Lucas knew what she was really saying: *Are you sure you're prioritising your son?*

By the time he'd greeted Hazel at the hospital, taken off his jacket and made himself a cup of tea he thought he had regrouped enough to be as present for his patients as he needed to be. The childminder was right. He'd leapt too far, too soon, with this whole Christmas thing with Kiara. His son was only three. He didn't need all the bells and whistles. Especially when there was confusion. He'd dial it back...maybe get Harry a snow globe or something to tide him over until the big day. And then, one day when Harry was older, they'd set about figuring out how to do Christmas their way. Whatever that was.

But when he opened the door to his surgery, his resolve to face the season on his own disintegrated instantly.

There, on the table, was a tiny living Christmas tree, all decorated, with a small handwritten note that said simply:

A starter tree for the two Wilde men in my life. K x

CHAPTER SEVEN

KIARA SHOWED HER patient the blood pressure gauge. 'We can do it again if you like, but I think it might stress you out more.' She released the cuff and untagged the Velcro from around the woman's arm. 'It is worth bearing in mind that one fifty-nine over one ten is edging on severely high.'

Audrey Keene gave her arm a rub where the cuff had been and blew out a breath that clearly didn't calm her in the slightest. The poor woman was all nerves.

'Would you like to call your husband?' asked Kiara.

'Can't.' She said briskly. 'He's away until Crimbo.'

'And he's out of touch until then?'

'Oil rigs. His is way out. He can send texts sometimes, but I don't want to tell him this in a text.' She pretended to type on her phone. *'Hey, babe. Your wife and child might be dead by the time you get back. Merry Christmas!'*

'Hey…' Kiara soothed. 'No. We've got this.'

She took the phone out of her patient's hand, put it on the desk, and then took both of Audrey's hands in hers. She looked her straight in the eye. This was her first child, and she was only young. Twenty-three. Having a husband who worked out on the oil rigs most of the year didn't help either.

'There are risks with any pregnancy but being aware of what's happening with you and the baby is half the battle. You're at the best midwifery centre in the area. And there's a hospital nearby if—'

'Hospital!'

Audrey paled further, and Kiara could actually see her pulse pounding in her throat. Oh, crumbs… Were they were heading for a panic attack?

'We're here now. Look at me, Audrey. Focus on my eyes. Breathe in and out. Nice and slow. That's it. Now, is there anyone else we can ring for you?'

Audrey pressed her lips together, then pushed them out, her face contorting as if she were about to cry. 'I'd really feel happier if my GP was aware of this.'

'Not a problem.' Kiara's heart went out to

Audrey. She picked up a pen. 'Just give me the number and I'll give them a ring as soon as we're done.

'I mean…' Audrey squeaked. 'Right now. I think we should tell them right now.'

Kiara and Audrey stared at the blood pressure machine. It was telling both of them the same thing. Audrey's blood pressure was way too high and she was potentially staring down the barrel of pre-eclampsia—something definitely worth avoiding. Professionally, Kiara knew she was spot-on with her diagnosis. And years of experience had taught her that trying to talk a frightened pregnant woman out of something when she was feeling alone and vulnerable was a bad idea.

'Not a problem,' she said again. 'Shall we get a urine sample and take a blood test first?' she suggested. 'That way we can give her a fuller picture of what's going on and—'

Audrey cut her off. 'My GP's a he—not a she.'

'Sorry.' Kiara pressed a hand to her chest. 'My bad. I shouldn't have assumed.'

Her thoughts instantly pinged to Lucas. She wondered, if he had become her GP, would she have wanted to stay with him because he was a good GP, or run for the hills.

Because how on earth could she tell him if she had…um…warts, for example? She didn't, but…

Her frown tipped into a smile as it occurred to her that Lucas was a man she could probably say anything to, no matter how embarrassing. He had a way about him. A calmness that assured her she wasn't being judged. Or dismissed. Or being kept in a tiny corner of his life so that he had plenty of room left to lead his real life.

In inviting her to help him steer through Christmas with Harry, he had invited her into the heart of his life, and she knew it had taken a lot of trust for him to do as much. Being with them brought her so much joy… Although maybe leaving the Christmas tree on his desk had been a step too far. There was hanging out together and there was inserting yourself into someone's life far more than they wanted.

Which was how Peter's wife had found out she existed. Kiara had made him a playlist and sent it to his phone. His wife had found it when she'd been going through his messages… The thought mortified her. If she'd been suspicious enough to be going through his phone messages, there was no chance Kiara had been his first affair. It was just too humiliating to think about.

She pushed the thoughts way back into the recesses of her mind and reminded herself that she'd only done the Christmas tree thing as her way of drawing a line in the sand. Or should that be putting a piece of tinsel on the snow?

Either way, whatever she thought had been buzzing between them hadn't been real.

She refocused on the situation at hand. Audrey and her high blood pressure. Pre-eclampsia was no joke, and they needed to get to the bottom of this.

Kiara softened her tone even further and, putting away the blood pressure equipment, said, 'Right, my dear. Are you happy to do bloods today? See if we can get a better picture of what's going on?'

'Um…' Audrey fretted her fingers into a weave, then shook them out as if they had ants on them and began tapping her index fingers against her chin as she spoke. 'Please don't think I'm only second-guessing you. I'm second-guessing everyone. You can't even begin to imagine what I'm putting my husband through. He was just home, and I'm pretty sure I'm the one who drove him back out to the rig. The poor man didn't know whether to buy me pickles or peanut butter or ice cream. No wonder he left!' Tears bloomed in her eyes and her voice lurched up an octave into a wail. 'I'm *impossible* to live with! How is he going to want to live with me when I have the baby?'

'Hey…' Kiara soothed, handing her a tissue as the tears began to fall. 'You're a mass of hormones. Don't give too much weight to the micro-moments. It's the big picture you need to keep in mind.'

It was advice she could do with listening to herself. Whenever she was near Lucas, she, too, was 'a mass of hormones'. A *mess*, more like. Especially as she had to keep reminding herself, *He's not available. His heart is already full and there's no room at the inn for you!*

As a result, teasing reality apart from fantasy after they'd spent the evening together had become her number one pastime. And the number one thing she'd tried not to think about at work.

Even so…

She curled one of her hands into the other, feeling her body instinctively pulling up the memory of Lucas taking her hand in his and giving it the lightest of squeezes. It could have meant nothing. It could have been an accident. It could have just been a friendly thank-you. Or it could have meant he was feeling that same electric connection she was every time they were together.

She looked from her hands to Audrey's and realised her patient's hands were trembling. 'Audrey, I'm here for you. I am your midwife and we've got this. We're going to do the tests and sort everything out—all right?'

'No!' Audrey snapped. 'No. It's *not* all right. *Nothing's* going to be all right.' A look came over her face that was almost frightening. 'I can't do this on my own. I never even have the right food in the house. How on earth am I going to grow this baby properly, let alone *have* the baby. What if I die? I might die!'

Audrey was definitely having a panic attack. Kiara wondered if she'd had more than one—hence the high blood pressure.

She got down on her knees in front of Audrey and covered her hands with her own. 'Audrey? Can you look at me please?'

Audrey began to shake her head back and forth, muttering something she couldn't quite make out. Her breathing was coming in short, sharp huffs now.

'Audrey? Audrey… I need you to look at me. We're going to slow down your breathing, otherwise you might get dizzy.'

Audrey kept murmuring the same thing. The words had a familiarity Kiara couldn't quite work out, until all of the sudden she heard it loud and clear: *'Dr Wilde.'*

'Is Dr Wilde your GP? Dr Lucas Wilde?' She had to keep repeating his name, all the while reminding herself that she shouldn't let it taste so sweet on her tongue.

Eventually she got a nod of affirmation out of her patient.

'Would you like to see him?' Kiara asked.

'Yes!' Audrey was all but pleading.

Kiara's body flooded with an energy that didn't know what to do with itself. She had a patient who needed help. From Lucas. The one man in the world Kiara loved to be with but also didn't. Because whenever she was with him her emotions took on a life of their own. One minute they were demanding she give him a Christmas tree. The next they were regretting it because of the ample opportunity to misread the gesture.

Was it friendly? Or over-friendly? An invitation to throw caution to the wind and see what all the crazy frissons buzzing between them were about? Or the total opposite? Which, of course, made a whole other set of feelings burst to the fore. Because whenever she looked into Lucas's eyes she felt something so much more powerful than anything she'd ever felt when she was with Peter. It terrified her—because how would she ever survive another broken heart?

She wouldn't. Not to mention the fact that there wasn't a storage unit large enough for all her Christmas things, let alone the decorations she had yet to buy. And, of course, she'd have to find a new place to live and a new job—which she didn't want because she completely loved it here. And Harry! She couldn't even get started on how she felt about Lucas's son, because just when she thought she'd tapped into the bottom of her emotional well, it became insanely apparent that there were fathoms of emotions yet to go.

'Kiara?' Audrey's expression was a mix of concern and confusion as she continued to fight for breath. 'Do you not like Dr Wilde?'

'No! I mean yes. Of course. Why would you ask that?'

'Your face has gone all funny.'

Kiara's cheeks burned with embarrassment, and she made a heroic effort to refashion her expression into something vaguely approaching professionalism—because her focus shouldn't ever have veered from Audrey.

See? This is why you don't get all gooey over colleagues who aren't available. You take your eyes off the ball and go into a tailspin whenever their names are mentioned.

She gave her spine a sharp wriggle and took hold of Audrey's hand again, all the while lobbing her swirling mass of mixed emotions into the ether. And hopefully beyond.

'Let's call him right now. He's only downstairs.'

She took the phone and coached Audrey through some more steadying breaths as she rang down to Reception.

'Hi, Hazel? Is there any chance you could put me through to Dr Wilde?'

Hazel said she'd just seen him heading to the break room—most likely for a cup of tea. 'Would you like me to fetch him for you, love?'

'Yes, please. And can you tell him it's quite urgent? It's about one of his patients.'

Right. Excellent. That was more like it. Patients first. Totally uncontrollable emotions squished. Job done.

* * *

Lucas flew up the stairs, skipping every other one. He had seen enough of Kiara at work to know she would only call for help if she really needed it. But if it was extremely urgent, there were people closer to hand than him.

Hazel hadn't mentioned who the patient was, and he could only guess that the omission meant Kiara was honouring patient confidentiality. Whoever it was, she must be one of his.

The door to her room opened just as he was about to knock.

Kiara's expression was focused and in control. Before she stepped aside, she quickly explained. 'I've got Audrey Keene with me. A discussion about her high blood pressure has escalated. I've been trying to steady her breathing, but she kept requesting you, so I thought I had better defer to the patient's wishes.'

He walked into the room with a nod of thanks as Kiara closed the door behind him.

Seeing her like this, charged with energy and drive, reminded him anew of just how fundamental a response he had to her. It wasn't just Christmas trees and dancing penguins that had drawn them together. It was more visceral than that. They were a match. In good times and, if her expression was anything to go by, in bad.

Before Kiara could say anything else, Audrey began wheezing. Lucas took two long-legged strides and was soon squatting down so that he was at eye level with her. 'Audrey? It's me. Dr Wilde.' To Kiara he said, 'Can you find me a small paper bag?'

She nodded and went straight to the supplies cupboard, returning seconds later with a plain white bag. After she'd handed him the bag, she scribbled something on a bit of paper and held it up out of Audrey's eye line.

Panic attack?

He nodded. Audrey had been prone to them even before she fell pregnant. He was surprised Kiara hadn't noticed the mention of them in her notes. He had definitely made a record of them. Then again, Kiara was new here. Perhaps Audrey had staggered in this way, already mid-flow. Or, more likely, they'd been going through her notes together as Kiara got up to speed and, unfortunately for Audrey, a case of the nerves had leapt to the fore.

'Audrey?' Lucas put a hand on her shoulder, 'It's Dr Wilde,' he repeated. 'Kiara and I are both here to help you. Did you come in this way? Feeling anxious?'

Audrey reached out a hand and gripped his, as if trying to physically channel some of his easy, steady breathing into her own lungs.

In a low, steady voice, Kiara said, 'Audrey came in to see Marnie, not realising she was on maternity leave. She and I came in here to go through her notes and I thought her blood pressure was a bit high.'

'What were the numbers?'

She told him, and in that same, low, steady voice went on, 'Her husband's away working and it doesn't sound like there's anyone else to ring. Do you think it might be something else? Should we run an ECG?'

He shook his head. 'Not just yet. But you're right. We should definitely do some tests before she leaves.' He added some sunshine to his voice and said to Audrey, 'Sometimes we take a little walk when things get too intense—don't we, Audrey?'

She was staring at him, wide-eyed with fear, one hand on her belly, one holding the paper bag to her mouth.

'That's right... Slow and steady... One... two...three...four... And hold for one... two... Excellent.' He sat back on his heels, listening as Audrey's breaths started to come in short staccato bursts again. 'Audrey? Kiara and I are concerned about you and the baby. We're going to breathe with you, okay? All three of us breathing together... One, two, three...'

After a few moments, Kiara shot him a look. It wasn't helping. Their eyes locked, and in the few seconds their gazes held they exchanged a raft of information. These short, sharp exhalations of hers were pushing all the CO_2 out of her body. The absence of CO_2 would make her blood more alkaloid, which would then kick off a domino effect on the metabolism of calcium, which she would feel in her hands, then her feet, and then, unless she could regain control, her heart.

'Shall we see if we can get you up and walking?'

Lucas took one of Audrey's hands in his and wrapped an arm around her shoulders as she pushed herself up and out of the chair with the other hand. He signalled with his eyes that Kiara should take Audrey's other hand, which she did, wrapping an arm around the back of her waist as she did so. Which was just as well, because the moment she rose out of the chair Audrey gave a precarious wobble.

They steadied her as if they were one, exchanging glances and unspoken thoughts as organically as if they'd worked together for years.

'Thank you for the Christmas tree,' he whispered as Audrey regrouped for a moment.

Kiara's eyes lit up in surprise and then softened with pleasure. She gave him a smiley nod but said nothing, pressing her lips tight together as if she was holding his thanks inside herself like a present.

Audrey began to pull at her collar, as if she were trying to get fresh air on herself. Beads of sweat began to present on her forehead.

'Audrey?' Lucas turned his full attention back on to their patient, an idea growing from seeing the gesture. 'Let's get outside in the sunshine, shall we?'

Audrey managed a nod, which was good. It was progress. It meant she was breathing slowly enough to be able to listen.

Lucas began to guide them towards the stairs, anxious that taking the lift might trigger more panic. Their progress was slow. From the looks some of their colleagues were throwing them, Lucas was beginning to wonder if he'd made the right call, but the first thing Audrey did when they finally were outside in the beautifully manicured gardens, lit golden by the winter light, was take a huge, relieved breath. As if it was being indoors that had been the source of her anxiety and nothing more.

Relief flooded through Kiara's features. She wore an expression which no doubt matched his own. It was always a tenuous call—leaving behind the myriad of machines they could hook her up to and the medicines they could give her to calm her down. But he knew Audrey well enough to go with his gut, and it had paid dividends.

He and Kiara pointed out various things in the garden: bright yellow winter jasmine, the colourful cyclamen beds, a low hedge made of orange and red dogwood boughs, glowing with the same colours. There were holly trees weighted with berries. And, of course, a huge evergreen, circled from bottom to top with fairy lights.

'Are you looking forward to Christmas, Audrey?'

Kiara's own excitement shone through, instantly bringing a smile to Lucas's face.

'I love the simplicity of this tree...' she pointed to the towering evergreen '...but I think Dr Wilde can confirm that my love of Christmas is...erm...'

'Not exactly subtle?' Lucas supplied, when Kiara failed to find a description of her glittering love of the festive season.

'Oh. My. Gawd.' Audrey stopped in her tracks, as if the entire panic attack had never happened at all, then threw up her hands and clapped them together as if she'd just discovered Kiara was a rock star. 'Do you live in that adorable cottage that looks as if it's straight out of the North Pole?' she asked.

'Guilty.'

'Why guilty?' Audrey looked at Lucas, as if trying to garner support. 'That place is pure magic! Right? I mean, I'm totally right. Magic,' she reiterated, with a stern look at Lucas as if daring him to contest her.

How could he? Kiara's love of Christmas was what had first put them in one another's path, and he had to admit this Christmas season so far had been his best in years—if not ever.

Lucas and Kiara shared a smile as Audrey began a long, detailed explanation of how much she adored Mistletoe Cottage, and how she'd been making sure to walk past it every day since the first set of decorations had gone up. It reminded her of her love of Christmas as a young girl, and she'd been hoping that whoever lived there would decorate it that way for ever, so she could walk her baby past, and then her toddler, and then hopefully, because of Mistletoe Cottage, her baby would love Christmas as much as she did.

Suddenly aware that she'd been gabbling on, she clapped her fingers to her mouth, pressing a giggle into submission. 'I'm sorry. I didn't— Hey!' She widened her hands and grinned at the pair of them. 'The panic attack is gone! Your Christmas cottage cured me!'

Laughing, the three of them headed back into the warmth of the hospital. Lucas noted that a swag of mistletoe had appeared in the doorway to the staff lounge as they made their way to Kiara's room.

'I'm happy to stay while Kiara takes your bloods and other stats,' Lucas began, but Audrey stopped him.

'I'm good. Kiara and I need to discuss the merits of seasonal glitter balls.'

'And you'll make sure to ring one of us if you ever feel panicky again?' he asked.

'Better than that!' Audrey beamed. 'I'm going to take myself on a walk to Mistletoe Cottage next time. How could I not relax, looking at all of that joy?'

Kiara grinned at him as she pumped up the blood pressure gauge, and to their collective delight he saw that it was significantly lower than it had been the first-time round.

Lucas headed to the door, but before leaving he ducked his head back in and asked Kiara, 'Hot chocolate later?'

She scrunched her nose. 'I can't.' She threw a look at Audrey, then explained, 'I'm having an open house tomorrow night.'

'Oh, yes. Of course. Harry ensured I put that on the calendar.' He was about to offer to help, but as Audrey was there decided now wasn't the time.

He gave her a wave goodbye just as Kiara was explaining to Audrey about the charity she was collecting money for, and then he heard Audrey's squeals of delight as Kiara started telling her about her festive cushion collection.

He hadn't realised how broadly he was smiling until he passed the main desk, where once again Nya was giving him that mischievous smile of hers. Rather than look bewildered, as he had before, this time he gave her a jaunty salute and danced what he hoped looked like a small but carefree Christmas jig.

CHAPTER EIGHT

Mince pies?

There were scores of the star-topped, sugar-dusted beauties, fresh out of the oven, covering every platter and plate Kiara owned.

Mulled wine?

Gallons of it. The warm, enticing scent of cinnamon, cloves and allspice was almost literally wrapping her house in an extra layer of magic.

She had even warmed up some apple juice as well, and lightly spiced it with cinnamon. And she'd made gingerbread men and put out bowls of nibbles just in case anyone happened to stay into the early evening.

She'd also put up countless more baubles, but...

She went outside to look at her cottage with fresh eyes. It was all there. The dancing penguins. The snowman and his pals. Stars. Candy canes. Huge gingerbread men. Even

Santa was up there on her roof now, courtesy of the man who'd come to adjust her television aerial the other day. And a few elves.

The decorative trees in her front garden had twirls of lights on them, as did all of the super-sized candy canes and the wicker reindeer. There were moving light displays too, that made it look as if the house was being softly blanketed by huge, decorative snowflakes. And there were fairy light angels who, when a button was pressed, sang Christmas carols. There were super-sized 'presents' and glittery bell baubles.

Every single Christmas decoration she could think of.

She had set up several fake gingerbread houses, which were actually coin collectors, at the front gate, by her front door and on the kitchen counter, all with pamphlets explaining about First Steps and why it was such a great charity. She'd already managed to collect an impressive amount of money in her little Santa's workshop donation box, and was hoping today would put her at her target goal.

But still there was something missing. And she didn't have a clue what it was.

Night fell early this time of year…in the afternoon, actually. And she had taken the day off especially to make sure her open house was truly open to the public by the time schools let out. She knew Harry and Lucas wouldn't be coming until later, but from the moment people started arriving—first in trickles, then in a steady flow—she simply couldn't stop scanning the crowd, looking for that tidily cropped head of brown hair attached to a man she knew she really shouldn't be falling for but, against her better judgement, had already fallen for.

'Kiara!'

Before she could register who had said her name, Kiara was being wrapped in the arms of a definitely pregnant woman. She realised it was Audrey, her patient from yesterday. She looked an entirely changed woman. Her dark hair was twisted up underneath an adorable knitted cap in green and white stripes with a line of reindeer knitted along the base and a huge gold bauble on top. Her cheeks glowed with health and her eyes were sparkling bright. But it was her smile that was the best thing to see.

Still holding on to one another's arms, they pulled back and grinned at one another. 'You look amazing,' they both said at the same time, then laughed.

More seriously, Kiara asked, 'Are you feeling all right?'

'Much better.' Audrey's voice was ripe with gratitude, and once again she pulled Kiara in for a hug. 'I can't thank you enough for everything you and Dr Wilde did for me.'

'Uh-oh! What have I done now?'

Lucas's buttery voice swept with warm caramelly magic down Kiara's spine, swirling and dreamily pooling in her tummy, where... Yes, there they were...the Christmas butterflies had taken flight.

Their eyes connected and that increasingly familiar buzz swept through her, as if a thousand fireflies were heralding the arrival of her soulmate.

Which, of course, was completely ridiculous.

He'd loved his wife. Who he couldn't be with any more. So he would not love another woman. No matter how right it felt when they were together.

Lucas's lips parted, his expression soft, as if he, too, was going through a similar internal checklist.

I like her, but I don't love her. I can't love her.

Before he could say anything, Lucas was

being wrapped in one of Audrey's heartfelt bear hugs.

'Kiara!' Harry appeared from around the other side of the picket fence and dropped his scooter, running and jumping up into her arms as if he'd done it a thousand times. He was wearing a knitted beanie that looked like a gingerbread man, his blond curls peeking out from beneath the hat and a bright red yarn bobble topping it all off. He looked adorable. And so, so lovable. She hugged him close, cherishing his little boy scent. She didn't care what the nursery rhymes said. This little boy smelt of sugar and spice and everything nice.

'Daddy!'

Kiara looked up to see that Lucas was standing in front of them, holding out his arms for his little boy.

'Here. I'll take him.' He was smiling, and his expression was kind, but there was something about the gesture that cut her to the quick. It was as if he was reminding her that Harry wasn't hers to love. Not in the way a mother would. Just like her ex's wife had.

You think you can have what we have? A family? You'll never have a family. You'll never know this kind of love.

Lucas's brow crinkled and he stepped in

closer. 'He's a bit heavy for you, isn't he?' He angled his head to try and meet her gaze. 'Kiara…?'

The movement, his proximity and the scent of him—juniper and pine—jarred her into action. 'Yes. Of course. You're right. I tell everyone I need to build up my upper body strength. Ha-ha! You'd think carrying babies around all day would do the trick, but nope!' She handed Harry over and gave her bicep a little squeeze. 'Nothing there but flimsy noodles! Protein…' She tapped the side of her nose in an attempt at a wise gesture. 'I have it on good authority that I should eat more protein.'

Oh, God. If the earth could open up and swallow her whole right now, she'd be nothing but grateful.

Lucas shifted Harry onto his hip and gave one of his little boy's hands a kiss before giving her a slightly perplexed smile. 'You don't need to change a thing, Kiara.' Lucas seemed genuinely confused by her peculiar monologue. 'You're perfect as you are.'

What? He thought she was perfect? No one in the history of her entire life had ever called her anything close to perfect. Did that mean—

Lucas made his voice bright and childish

as he gave Harry's hand a jiggle. 'Isn't she Harry? We wouldn't want our new friend any other way.'

'Happy…happy!' sing-songed Harry.

Of course. Perfect as a friend. Well, that was her solidly placed in the Friend Zone.

A sinkhole clearly wasn't going to help her out here. Panic began to grip her chest in the same way she'd seen it take hold of Audrey yesterday. But this was not the time or place to have any sort of meltdown.

Having her emotions split into a kaleidoscope of conflicting emotions by a man who had unwittingly swept into her heart and made her feel whole again was a brandnew level of heartache she wished she didn't know existed.

'Um… Mince pies.' She pointed randomly over her shoulder and then said, 'Apple juice,' before quickly excusing herself, refusing to register the bewildered expression playing across Lucas's face as she turned away and quickly absorbed herself into the crowd.

An hour later, as the crowd began to clear, Lucas appeared in front of her with a broom and dustpan and a very sleepy Harry at his side. 'I thought maybe we could help you clean up.' Harry unleashed a huge, unprotected yawn. Lucas gave him a fond look.

'And by "we" I mean me. Any chance I could put this guy in the spare room for a nap?'

'Oh, gosh…' She pulled a face. 'You don't have to stay and help. That's ever so kind—'

Lucas held up a hand. 'It's the least we can do after all the joy you've brought us.'

Harry leant against his father's leg and wrapped his arms around it, looking as if he might fall asleep on the spot. The complication of emotions she'd felt earlier suddenly lost their relevance. How could they be relevant when Harry so clearly needed to be sleeping? Besides… Even though adrenaline was still running through her from an evening spent mostly trying to avoid Lucas, she had to admit an extra set of hands to help with the clearing up would be genuinely useful.

They cleaned the place as if they had been doing it together for years. Intuitively knowing when the other person needed a hand or when it would be all right to head off to another room and tidy up there.

'Gosh!' Kiara looked around her living room with a smile. 'It looks as good as new.'

She smiled at Lucas, who was standing by her wood basket. He was so handsome. So kind. It tore at her heart that she had found someone so perfect to love and yet her love was so destined to be unrequited. A loneliness crept into her bones. She didn't want to give it space, but despite her best efforts to push it away she shivered.

'Shall I pop a couple of logs on the fire?' Lucas asked.

'That'd be nice. Kiara smiled in gratitude and then, suddenly wanting more than anything not to have this moment end, blurted, 'You wouldn't want to stay for a quiet glass of wine and a final mince pie, would you? Something to fortify you before carrying that son of yours home.'

What the *hell*? Had she gone *mad*?

The good fairy on her shoulder—the responsible one—was looking at her as if she'd just grown an extra head. Women who'd had their hearts crushed by one married man did not invite emotionally unavailable sexy dads to stay and drink wine on their sofa with them.

That naughty fairy—the one who was greedy and wanted to spend just a few quiet moments with Lucas before she officially called the evening to a close—didn't think there'd be much harm in just one more glass of mulled wine by the fire, with only the twinkling lights of the tree lighting up the room…

The good fairy prepared herself to stage an intervention.

'That sounds like a great idea.'

Lucas was already putting logs on the fire, and from this angle she had a really good view of his very pinchable bum.

He turned back and smiled at her. 'Thoughtful of you to give Harry some extra sleeping time.'

Ha! Yes. Totally *not* what she'd been thinking. But she made a vague noise, indicating that that had definitely been her intention.

She was going to make a joke about trying to lift a sleeping Harry and failing, but thought better of it. Rehashing her more humiliating moments in front of the man she wished she could love was an exercise in self-defeatism she didn't need to subject herself to.

She bustled around a bit, until finally presenting Lucas with a plate laden with mince pies, some cheese and crackers, as well as the promised glass of wine.

He noticed she was now empty-handed. 'You're not having anything?' he asked.

Unlike the first time her ex, Peter, had taken her to the pub, and she'd agreed not only to a second but a third glass of wine, this evening the imaginary good fairy had proactively taken her by the shoulders and shaken her when she'd pulled a second glass from the cupboard just now. Tipsy and besotted were not a good combination. Not for her. Not at any time of year. But especially not at Christmas. And super-especially not with Lucas Wilde sitting on her sofa looking like the Christmas card of her dreams.

She shook her head. 'I have enough Christmas cheer running though me already.' She pointed back at the kitchen, where the kettle was coming to a boil. 'I'm on the herbal tea now. Christmas spice.'

She waggled her hands and Lucas laughed. 'Leave it to you to find Christmas tea. What is it? Gingerbread-flavoured?'

'Close!' Her voice matched his playful tone, and despite her effort to keep herself in the Friend Zone she heard herself walking a fine line between fun and flirtation. 'Spiced apple.'

'Sounds good.' He rubbed his tummy.

And, as ridiculous as it was, she loved the homeliness of the gesture. It was so Papa Bear.

To stop herself from throwing herself at him, ripping his shirt off and begging him to tell her if his emotional landscape was as tumultuous and horny as hers, she went back to the kitchen and stuffed her head in the freezer for a count of ten deep breaths.

But even that didn't work. As she prepared her tea, and a small plate of snacks, she let an image of the two of them as a couple slip into her mind. Right here in Mistletoe Cottage. It was still decorated for Christmas, but maybe not quite to the level she'd done it this year. They'd have just had a dinner party, maybe. Or, like tonight, a neighbourhood open house, ripe with laughter and community spirit. They'd be keeping their voices low as Harry slept, aware of his building excitement for Christmas. Come Christmas Eve they'd be hanging three stockings by the chimney with care. Laying out surprise Christmas presents. Curling up on the sofa together...

She balled her hands into fists and mentally tried to knock some sense back into her head. Being with Lucas wasn't her reality, and it definitely wouldn't be her future.

'You're the one who invited him to stay, but it isn't your fault he said yes and then looked all sexy and desirable,' said the naughty fairy.

'You're the one who will sit at the opposite end of the sofa and eat mince pies with him and talk about the joys of getting urine

samples...then stand as far away as possible as you wave him off when he and his son go back to their own home. Their real home,' said the sensible fairy.

'That plan is stupid,' said the naughty fairy, pouting.

'Everything all right?'

Lucas was at the doorway, concern creasing his features as he took in the mad vision of Kiara clutching her head. And very possibly talking to herself.

'Good! Fine! I—' she began, and then, hoping her parents wouldn't mind, she covered the moment with a half-truth. 'Just missing my family, that's all.'

Lucas pressed one of his hands to his chest in a gesture of undiluted empathy. 'I hear you... It can really hit you out of the blue this time of year, can't it?'

She nodded, grateful that he understood. And doubly grateful that they now had a sort of neutral topic to discuss. One that wasn't about the two of them, anyway.

Lucas crossed over to her and picked up her plate, the gentle waft of his man scent obliterating anything the sensible fairy had suggested from what was left of her brain.

'C'mon. Grab your tea and let's get you settled on the sofa for a well-deserved break.'

When he turned his back to lead the way into the living room, Kiara feigned a swoon. How could someone so perfect be so far out of reach?

Because he's not meant to be yours. So suck it up and eat a mince pie.

Kiara settled on the sofa, popping a Santa face cushion on her lap to stand in as a table. When she looked up to find him looking at her, a rush of shyness swept through her. They'd never sat like this before and just… talked. There was always some sort of festive buzz happening around them. Or work things. It didn't surprise her, though, to realise that it felt as natural as if they'd been doing it for years.

'Does your family do a big Christmas?' she asked, after a few moments of contented munching.

Lucas shook his head. 'Not so much these days.'

Kiara nodded, more interested in what he wasn't saying than what he was. 'Is that recent?'

He gave a forlorn huff of a laugh. 'If you mean is it since Lily died? No. It was before that. I guess the Wilde family were never really wild about Christmas.' He quirked an eyebrow at her. 'See what I did there?' He waved off his silly pun, then explained more seriously, 'My parents retired to France a few years ago, and my sisters go there for Christmas. Lily's parents took to going on cruises once the children had flown the coop, and I was usually working right up until "the big day", so I never made too much of an effort to get down to France. And once the little guy was born… I guess it was just another excuse to stay put. Sort things out as best we could.'

Kiara frowned. 'Do you all get on? Your families?' She shook her head. 'Sorry… That's quite a personal question.'

'Oh, yes we do.' His response was genuine. 'Seriously, I didn't mean to give you any "crazy family" vibes. I suppose we're more significant birthday types than Christmas types, that's all.' He leant forward to give her knee a tap and his smile warmed. 'I think this is the first year I can genuinely say I have been properly infused with the Christmas spirit.'

Despite her silent warning to herself that this was just a friendly chat, she blushed, flattered to the core by the compliment. And then the rush of feelings she'd been trying to keep at bay swept in and filled her body with a warm glow she never wanted to shake.

And why should she?

Here she was, on the sofa with a man she admired and was stupidly attracted to. His son was sleeping peacefully in the spare room. A fire was crackling away. There was wine and herbal tea and snacks, and the energy of a genuinely gorgeous evening all around them, but...

Sensible fairy piped up. *'Your heart will be broken in the end, Kiara. Pull the plug now.'*

'Are you happy here?' Lucas asked.

He'd thought she must be, but there was something that was suddenly missing in that soft smile of hers. *Her eyes*, it occurred to him. *The light hasn't reached her eyes.*

She thought for a moment before she answered, and when she did her voice was steady, but it bore an undercurrent of emotion that lifted and rose into her cheeks. 'I love my house.' She grinned and put her hands out, as if she were a model in a showroom. 'I also love my job and my colleagues,' she said in a more heartfelt manner, and then, as if realising he was one of her colleagues, she looked away and sighed.

'What?'

He tipped his head to one side and looked at her. Really looked at her. She was such a beautiful woman. Sitting here in the glow of the firelight, with the lights from outside the window providing a soft fairy lit warmth around her. It was a reflection on her overall aura. She was a kind woman whose personality instantly drew people to her. She'd lived here less than a month and already she had the entire village eating out of her hand. In contrast, he'd come into town under the radar. On purpose.

Everyone loved Mistletoe Cottage and its dazzling decor. And the fact that she was doing it all for charity. They loved *her*. But he could see now, in this moment of vulnerability, that she wasn't as brave as she seemed. Nor as happy. And that cut him to the quick. This was a woman whose heart was so generous, so empathetic. She deserved all the happiness she desired, and yet something was keeping her from attaining it.

A need gripped him to do anything he could to help. 'There's something missing, though, isn't there?' he asked. 'Is it your family? The distance from London?'

She shook her head, her smile tinged with melancholy. 'No. I love my parents, but I moved out of their house years ago, so we're used to living our independent lives. Although we talk all the time. No, it's more...'

She picked at the tufty white beard sown onto her Santa cushion and then gave an embarrassed smile. 'It's more they thought I'd be married by now. Having children. Setting up house. The whole nine yards, as they say.'

'And you? Is that what you thought?'

She met his gaze. 'I thought so as well.'

There was something about the way she said it that suggested she'd been on track for exactly that, but it had been stolen from her. 'Was there someone specific you thought you'd be married to?' he asked.

She turned crimson.

He was feeling the heat of the question as well. It wasn't his business, and he wasn't even certain he wanted to know the answer. The idea of Kiara, dressed as a bride, walking down the aisle towards someone who—well, someone else, tugged at a part of him that hadn't seen oxygen in years.

She took a sip of her tea and then, as if having made a decision, set it down and looked him square in the eye. 'I did have a boyfriend. We were together for three years.'

'Sounds serious...' Lucas took a sip of wine and then put it to one side. He didn't want to get tipsy listening to this story. He wanted to be as present for her as she had been for him when he'd told her about Lily.

She nodded in acknowledgement of his comment, then continued in a way that suggested she hadn't talked about this in a while—if ever. As if she needed to get it out quickly…as if letting the words loiter in her body for a moment longer than necessary would cause her physical pain.

'He worked at the same hospital as me. He was—is—a surgeon.'

Her brow crinkled, as if remembering caused her pain. Lucas wanted to reach out to her, comfort her, but he knew this was a story she needed to tell from the safe nook of her sofa, with her cushion taking the blows as her fingers clenched and unclenched against it.

'We flirted at work, and that led to drinks afterwards, which led to…other things. And soon enough we were an item. Our schedules were always busy, so it was a bit haphazard as far as a traditional courtship goes. I'm sure you can imagine…'

Her eyes flicked to him, as if hoping for an acknowledgement but not a judgement, so he nodded. He understood. Surgeons worked mad hours, as did midwives. Babies didn't keep to a nine-to-five schedule.

'Anyway…' she continued. 'We did some of the normal boyfriend-girlfriend stuff. Dinner dates. He met my friends. He met my parents. They thought he was brilliant. My mother kept saying things like, "Our daughter...marrying a surgeon!'" She pulled a face, as if to say they'd been as deluded as she had.

Lucas felt ire raise in him. Whoever the hell this guy was, he certainly hadn't deserved Kiara. And no way did she deserve to hold this amount of pain and, if he wasn't mistaken, shame.

'We had weekends away and so on. But we never spent Christmas together. Last Christmas I asked him—*again*—if maybe this year we'd be spending Christmas together, and again he put off making a final decision. Later that night my phone rang.' Saying the words seemed physically painful for her. 'It was his wife.'

She paused for effect, but he could see tears bloom in her eyes. He ached to go to her. Move in close and wipe them away and curse this creep of a man who'd led her on. It was cruel, what he'd done to her.

Kiara's face was pure anguish as a solitary tear trickled down her cheek. 'I had no idea. If I'd had even the slightest of clues that he was married...'

She couldn't finish the sentence, succumbing to long-held-off sobs.

Lucas no longer checked his instincts. He moved across the sofa and held her close to him. He didn't offer trite words of consolation that wouldn't mean anything. Instead he just let her cry, expel the grief that she'd so clearly held inside.

Eventually, when the tears had gone, she pulled back and said, 'The worst part is, my parents don't even know.'

'What? Why not?'

'I was too ashamed.' She buried her head in her hands, then peeked out between her fingers. 'I was too humiliated to tell them that the man I'd been so cock-a-hoop for was a liar. Not to mention his poor family. I mean—he has *children*!' Her eyes flicked to the corridor which led to the room where Harry was sleeping.

Lucas's heart slammed against his ribcage. He felt humbled and moved that she should be thinking of others before herself when she had been so very wronged.

'He was a con man,' Lucas said indignantly. 'He took advantage of you. He was only thinking of himself. No one else. You can't possibly blame yourself for his selfish, heartless inconsideration.'

Kiara dropped her hands from her face, tears still glittering in her eyes. 'I just feel so stupid, you know…? Those first few months after we broke up I went over and over everything, trying to figure out if there had been signs. Things I should have noticed. Like him not ever wanting to share Christmas with me.' She huffed out a laugh that—incredibly—wasn't embittered.

His heart went out to her. 'A man like that—' he began, and then stopped himself. Slandering someone he didn't know wasn't the point. Ensuring Kiara knew that this wasn't her fault and that she should not carry one ounce of the burden of guilt was. 'You are not to blame. He presented himself as a man who was available.'

Kiara cringed. 'But seriously… After three Christmases, when he knew how much I loved Christmas, why wasn't I able to figure it out?'

Lucas thought of the last two years, when he hadn't been able to see the joy in the festive season no matter how much he had tried to talk himself into a bit of Christmas cheer. In little more than the blink of an eye Kiara had effortlessly all but transformed it for both him and Harry. She'd made this season that he found so troubling a time of generosity and joy. It was fun! She was a woman who should be made to feel amazing for the happiness she brought to people. And, of course, at work she brought calm. She was a rare breed of woman, and it killed him that someone had made her feel otherwise.

'You're a good person, Kiara. You didn't deserve to be treated like that.'

She blinked up at him, her lashes stained pitch-black with spilt tears. 'Thank you for not judging me.'

'Of course not,' he whispered. 'It wasn't even an option. Listen…' He took her hands in his and rubbed his thumbs along the back of them. 'You're one of the most extraordinary women I have ever met. If it were two hundred years ago I would definitely be threatening a duel with this scoundrel!'

His bravura won a smile and a hiccoughing laugh from her, which melted his heart even more. He liked being the man who'd brought that smile to her lips. His eyes dropped to her mouth and remained on it. She looked down, then back up at him. The atmosphere between them shifted in that instant. Energy surged from the pair of them and met in the ever-decreasing space between them.

He became acutely aware of her presence in his arms. The fabric of her Christmas jumper…the curve of her arm beneath it. The shift of her shoulder blades. The cadence of her pulse. He felt her as she presented to him: as a woman.

He'd often wondered about this moment. The one where he'd take a step away from his past and towards a different future. One he had never entirely been able to imagine. But maybe that was what life would be like with Kiara. One welcome surprise after the other.

Though his pulse had quickened, and his body had begun to feel heat travelling in darts of approbation to areas that hadn't been lit up for a long time, the moment also felt perfectly natural. It was as if she had belonged here in his arms all along, but that they'd each needed to follow the paths life had put them on to eventually guide them to one another.

Sweeping aside a few strands of hair that had stuck to her tear-streaked face, Lucas closed the space between them, feeling their shared energy come to fruition in an explosion of heat as their lips connected in a long-awaited kiss.

CHAPTER NINE

KIARA DIDN'T KNOW if she was in heaven, on earth, or in some magical place in between. Wherever it was, she didn't want to leave.

This was the stuff of fantasy.

A glittering Christmas tree. A heartfelt, meaningful talk with a man she was not only attracted to, but whom she respected. A man who not only refused to pass judgement, but who openly wanted to champion her. To kiss her!

The moment his lips touched hers she felt as if the final piece of the year-long puzzle she'd been piecing together had been completed. Cornwall plus Carey Cove plus Lucas was everything she'd ever wanted.

'You all right?' Lucas whispered against her lips.

'Mmm…' was all she managed.

Kissing Lucas was like finding herself anew. There was no comparing him to any other. Nor being drawn back to a time and place where she'd been in another man's arms. A man who had made her feel the very worst kind of humiliation. She'd thought she would panic if a man ever tried to kiss her again, but Lucas's kind words had served as a balm to the thoughts that had kept her up more nights than she cared to acknowledge.

The pain of discovery and subsequent fall-out had taken a physical toll on her. She hadn't realised how fragile she'd felt, starting this new existence. How much courage it had taken to sell up, find a new job, move across the country and start again...and not in a mild, self-recriminating way. In a way that announced who she was and how she wanted to live her life. And, against the odds, it had led her to Lucas. A man who had borne his own heartache and, if his tender touch was anything to go by, who was also looking for a foothold on a new future.

A shiver of delight whispered down her neck when Lucas traced his finger-pads along her cheeks as if he had mandated himself with a mission: to explore her, inch by careful inch.

'You're so beautiful,' he murmured as he ducked his head to the soft crook between her ear and her chin, dropping velvety kisses along her neck.

Her body absorbed his attention like sunlight. His fingertips traced her jawline, the backs of his palms brushed the fine hairs of her cheek and his soft stubble grazed her delicate skin as his lips touched, explored, tasted...

But each time she tried to take the reins, return the exquisitely detailed attentions he was giving her, he'd murmur, 'No. Me first. I want to know everything about you.'

It was a level of care she hadn't realised she'd hungered for. As if being cherished was an essential nutrient she'd not known she'd been missing all along. Vitamin Lucas.

No. Not even that was right.

He didn't complete her. He made her life better. And that was the key difference. Another person didn't make you whole...they admired you for everything you were and didn't hold you to ransom for the things you weren't.

The nanosecond of dark thought she'd permitted to enter her system must have translated into hesitation to him. He pulled back, his expression wreathed in concern. 'Are you sure this is all right?'

It was more than all right. It was soul-quenchingly delicious.

'Yes,' she said, cupping his cheeks in her hands and looking him straight in the eye. 'More than.'

'Good.' He pulled her to him and drew a long, luxurious kiss from her. The kind that made time irrelevant.

'And you're okay?' she asked, when a natural pause introduced itself.

It was important to her to check. This was as much a first for Lucas as it was for her. Just as importantly, Lucas didn't just have himself to think about. He also had to consider his son, sound asleep in her guest room.

'I'm okay,' Lucas assured her, running his fingers through her hair and down her back.

The sensation was both new and familiar all at once. As if he'd been doing it for years and might for years yet to come.

'Better than okay.' His smile was warm. Genuine. 'Best Christmas party I've ever been to.'

This time his smile was wicked. The lights reflected in those grey eyes of his glimmered with something more heated than she'd seen there before.

If someone had told her she was made of

starlight and fairy dust right now she would have believed them.

Her response to Lucas went beyond the elemental aspects of their very obvious chemistry. He *appreciated* her. And, more importantly, he wanted to make sure she knew it. Not to make her feel lucky that she'd been graced with his presence, as her ex had. She refused to allow herself to feel that shame again, even as she recalled how desperate she'd been for his attention. How grateful she'd felt when he'd deigned to shine his light on her. She saw it clear as day now. Her ex had been an arrogant, self-serving, egocentric jerk. His pleasure hadn't been to make her happy. His pleasure had been to hold power over her and his wife. Doling out his attentions as if they were fine gifts.

She felt a shift in her body chemistry as Lucas pulled her closer into his arms. *This* was genuine affection. This was what being cared for felt like. This was what she had wanted all along.

She untangled her limbs from his and, when he protested, put her index finger on his lips and said, 'My turn.'

She was smaller than him, so arranging herself on his lap so that her legs wrapped around him was not a problem. When she wriggled her hips and bottom into place her lips twitched with delight as Lucas gave a low moan of satisfaction. She reached for the top button of his shirt, desperate to feel her skin on his. He caught her hand in his, giving the back of it a kiss as his eyes darted to the corridor.

'Is there somewhere more private?' he asked.

The implication of his question exploded in her like lava. He wanted more.

She rose from the sofa and held her hand out to him. 'Follow me.'

Lucas felt more alive than he had in years. As if he could pinpoint each cell in his body and tell it where to direct its focus. His energy levels were soaring, as if they were absorbing the hyper-real sensations coursing through his bloodstream.

It was, he realised, the power of two.

Two hearts. Two minds. Two people attracted to one another on multiple levels.

Sight. Sound. Touch. All his sensory capabilities were focused on one thing: Kiara.

Holding her in his arms without a stitch of fabric between them was on another level. As if he'd never touched warm, soft skin before.

Being with her was nothing like what he'd

thought making love to someone who wasn't Lily would feel. Truth be told, he'd not let himself consciously consider being intimate with another woman. But, courtesy of his deeply erotic dream, being with Kiara felt more natural than he could have imagined. As if the dream had somehow prepared him for this different realm of pleasure with a woman.

There was no point in comparing, he'd realised, as slowly and purposefully they had taken one another's clothes off. They were both adults. People with pasts. With experience. And yet…this felt brand-new. As if the slate hadn't been washed clean, exactly— their histories would always be a part of them—but more as if one chapter had ended and another had begun.

He groaned in equal measures of loss and pleasure as Kiara pulled away from him, then made it clear it wouldn't be for long. She twirled her finger, indicating he should lie on his back, then slowly walked to the end of the bed where she stood, her brown eyes scanning the length of him as if he were a Christmas present she'd never imagined receiving.

She climbed onto the mattress on all fours, hovering over his legs and then, tantalisingly, his midsection. He was leaving her in no doubt that he desired her. She bent at the elbows, her breasts brushing the length of his chest as she swept her body along his, eventually lowering her lips to his for a hot, succulent kiss that magnetically arched their bodies against one another.

If the beginning of this chapter was anything to go by, he never wanted it to end.

Kiara pulled back a little…just enough so that the feather-soft warmth between her legs slid along the length of his erection. She was ready for him. If she wanted him.

Her eyes met his, as if asking him the same question, and there was only one answer. Yes. A thousand times yes. He wanted her as much as she seemed to want him.

She pushed herself up, her hands reaching for his. Their fingers wove together as the tip of his shaft met the heat of her feminine essence. The contact shot flames through him. It wasn't the length of time between now and the last time he'd made love…it was the intensity of the sensation, incinerating everything he'd used to be and rebuilding him into this new version of himself. He felt desired in a way he'd never known before. Cared-for. Appreciated fully for the man he was today.

It was an extraordinary feeling. Knowing

he was made of so many elements different from the person he'd once been awed him. And that he was sharing it with this woman—this beautiful, kind, incredible woman—was as humbling as it was empowering. He came with baggage. A lot of it. But today he felt as if he could handle it all. The past, the present and, more importantly, the future.

Time took on an otherworldly type of energy. The air around them was charged with more than oxygen. There was hunger…and need. And yet there wasn't any urgency about it. No voraciousness. There was a softness to their movements. A smouldering, slow burn shared between two people who wanted one another but felt no crush of pressure to do everything all at once. As if hurrying things would take away from the intensity of each touch and caress they shared.

After a delectation of time, they seamlessly moved and shifted into place, teasing and pleasuring each other to the point that he had a physical need to feel himself inside her. He confessed to not having any protection. She whispered that she was on the pill.

They exchanged a look. One charged with purpose and intent. Heated by desire. But their decision to go forward was a deliberate one, and that made the emotional impact of it even larger. He wanted her in a way he'd never wanted a woman before, and with her nod of consent he let the rest of the world fade away into nothing so that it was just the two of them.

He placed his hands on her hips and, after checking once again that she was happy to be with him like this, guided her down the length of himself.

His body was bombarded with sensations. Heat. Liquid pleasure. Movement undulating like the sea. It was a rhythm he realised he was participating in as Kiara rocked her hips in sync with his, their fingers woven together, their eyes locked on each other's, until at last he sat up and pulled her close to him, her taut nipples grazing his bare chest as he said, 'Wrap your legs around me.'

He didn't need to repeat himself. With a reserve of strength he hadn't realised he possessed, he picked her up and reversed their positions, so that he was on top. With her legs still around his waist he began to slowly recapture the rhythm, as if it had become a part of him. A part of them both.

Neither of them spoke again. It didn't seem necessary. All the time he'd spent with Kiara seemed to have built to this—a pure, unadulterated connection. He felt the intensity grow in him, and with it a shift in Kiara's energy, as if she felt it, too.

They clung to one another as their bodies took over. Movement overpowered thought as they merged into one beautiful, shared sensation of pleasure which built moment by moment until it did, finally, become urgent. The swell of accumulated potency finally reached its pinnacle and waves of pleasure washed through them both. The strength of their shared orgasm seemed inevitable and yet also to take them by surprise.

After a few moments Lucas lay down beside her and held her close, her heartbeat translating through to his until, after some long, lingering kisses, the pair of them fell asleep.

Before Kiara even opened her eyes she knew something was different about her bedroom. It wasn't that Lucas was there—because there was no way the evening they'd just shared wasn't going to be imprinted on her mind for ever. It was that he wasn't.

An icy slick of fear shot through her, holding her heart's ability to beat properly in its arctic hold. She forced herself to be still. To listen. Perhaps it wasn't that at all. Perhaps…

Again a glacial wave of panic swept through her as flashbacks to all the mornings she'd woken up alone came back to her. Mornings alone that she now knew hadn't been due to her ex's calls to the surgery ward, but to his family home.

No. Stop it. Lucas isn't like that. He let his son stay here, for heaven's sake.

She forced herself to take a slow breath, calming her hammering heart enough to let her listen to any sounds that might be coming from beyond her closed door.

Perhaps he'd thought a nice cup of tea in bed would be a lovely way to cap off a magic night. Or coffee? A mince pie? She sniffed the air for hints of any or all three. Listened for the tell-tale rumble of the kettle. The clink of spoons on the big chunky mugs she'd bought. The ones with Christmas trees and Santa faces and—her and Harry's favourite—the one with Rudolph the Red-Nosed Reindeer.

There was one sound. But it wasn't from the kitchen. It was the sound of a little boy, still drowsy and confused.

Shockwaves of fear reverberated through her. What was happening?

She pulled on some thick flannel pyjamas and a dressing gown and ran out into the corridor and downstairs where, in her small entryway, she saw Lucas zipping Harry into his winter coat.

He looked up but said nothing. He didn't need to. His expression said it all.

He regretted his night with her.

She stumbled back a step, the humiliation hitting her like an avalanche of pain. She'd thought she'd moved on from her past. Learnt her lessons. Buried her shame and remorse at having been so unwittingly played. But she hadn't. She hadn't come even close. It had all been right there, just below the surface, waiting for her.

Something must've played across her features and spoken to Lucas, because out of the silence and through the roar of blood pounding through her head she could hear him muttering something about nursery, change of clothes, a bath…

They were all legitimate reasons to take his son home. Definitely. But before he'd even woken up? The poor little boy was leaning against his father, half asleep, as Lucas fitted on him first one boot and then another. The sweetest little pair of boots that until now Kiara hadn't realised she'd loved seeing lined up next to her bigger boots and, next to them, Lucas's even larger ones. It had made her little cottage look more like a home than a dream. A hope.

And that was when it really hit her. This beautiful cottage that she loved so much, that she'd lavished with Christmas decor and scented candles and cushions and more fairy lights than the rest of the homes in Cornwall put together... She could have given all the money directly to charity rather than spending it on blinging up her house on the premise of raising awareness. She'd been showboating after all. Advertising her hunger to be a part of something. Anything, really. And the mortification that she'd been so public about her loneliness threatened to crush her.

'I'll see you later at Carey House?'

She saw the comment form on his lips... was not even certain she'd heard it. He certainly didn't mean in a romantic context. They wouldn't be dipping into the supplies cupboard and having a quick snog. Not the way this was going.

'Sure,' she managed. 'Of course.'

'And are you all right if we...you know... keep last night between us?'

He had the grace to wince at his request, but there was no chance he could know just how much it hurt her.

She couldn't begrudge him his behaviour. Not on a logical front. He was a widower with a young son to think of. Harry's welfare was paramount, and dragging him round the village on one-night stands was definitely not how Lucas operated. Even through her pain she knew this to be true. He might not want her any more, but he wasn't a cruel man. And she couldn't hold him to ransom for being the same level of Machiavellian as her ex.

But it didn't make it hurt any less. Or ease the pain she felt. With an apologetic flick of his eyes, he lifted his son into his arms and opened the door… The cold air was a mirror of the cold blood running through her veins.

The moment the door closed behind them she let the truth settle into her bones.

She was going to be someone's dirty little secret again.

How she'd managed to get into work that morning was a complete mystery.

'Everything all right?'

She stopped in the entryway, turned and saw Hazel's expression laced with concern.

'Fine!' She forced herself to give a bright smile, then tapped her head. 'Just…you know…recovering from yesterday.'

'Too much mulled wine?' Hazel asked with a knowing grin.

Kiara smiled back. She'd seen Hazel make a couple of return trips to the punch bowl as well. But she'd also seen her drinking water, and excusing herself to get home for 'something sensible to eat' afterwards.

The fact she was here with a smile on her face indicated that Hazel knew when enough was enough. Something Kiara wished she knew about falling in love. Because that was what had been happening to her these past few heady days. She'd been falling in love with Lucas—and with Harry—even though there was a part of her that had known all along that she shouldn't.

They weren't hers to love. They were on their own journey. One that didn't include her. Not in public, anyway. Not for Lucas. And there was no way she wanted to be someone's dirty little secret again.

'I've got some paracetamol if you need any...' Hazel began to dig in the reception desk drawer.

'No, no...' Kiara took a couple of steps up the stairs towards the midwives' lounge but then, remembering her manners, turned to offer a smile of thanks. The kind of pain she was enduring wouldn't respond to any kind of medication.

At just that moment Lucas came through the front door.

She froze in panic.

'Good morning, Dr Wilde!' Hazel greeted him cheerily. 'And how are we this morning? Full of festive cheer?'

Kiara almost physically felt the flash of panic that crossed Lucas's face.

Oblivious, Hazel danced knowing looks between the pair of them.

As if he was literally drawing a line under the days they'd spent together, Lucas said, 'Oh, you know… That's more Harry's department. Christmas isn't really my thing.'

And there it was in a nutshell. The addition of the insult to the injury. He might as well have had the message printed on a banner and flown it across the sky for the impact it had. She'd been a fool to fall for him. He'd only done all this for his son's sake. Played along. The kiss and then the lovemaking had all been a mistake. *She'd* been a mistake.

And as the true impact of what she'd done hit her she turned and took the stairs two at a time, unwilling to let him see just how much the loss of him had devastated her.

CHAPTER TEN

'MAKE SURE YOU take them every day—all right, Mr Thomas?'

Lucas's patient screwed up his face as if he'd just spoken to him in Martian.

'He will. My poor man can't hear without his hearing aids, and he didn't want to wear them—what with the infection and all.' Mrs Thomas gave her husband's leg a pat and then shouted, 'You'll be taking your medicine every day!' She tapped the prescription Lucas had just handed them. 'Right up until Christmas Eve.' She turned to Lucas; her face suddenly stricken. 'Will that mean no Christmas cheer for him?'

Lucas made a remorseful expression. 'I'm afraid not. Not with antibiotics.'

'Oh, well!' Mrs Thomas turned to her husband again, turning her speaking volume up to eleven. 'It's a good thing we went out to

Mistletoe Cottage for the mince pies and mulled wine—isn't it, love?'

Lucas rubbed his chin…hastily shaven and with a couple of nicks. Something he hadn't done in a long time. He didn't remember seeing the couple there. Which shouldn't come as a surprise to him. He'd only had eyes for Kiara.

The thought stung as an image of her face when she'd seen him this morning, a wretched mix of fear and sorrow, flashed across his mind's eye.

Mr Thomas grinned. 'It certainly is.' He patted his tummy. 'Those were the finest mince pies I've had in yonks. And imagine… eating them for charity!' A look of panic zapped across his face. 'I mean, they were the finest apart from *yours*, love. Obviously.' He leant across and gave his wife's sweet, dried apple face a kiss.

Mrs Thomas's features softened. She put her palm on her husband's cheek and then gave it a gentle pat before turning to Lucas with a happy smile. 'Forty-seven years of marriage and I've finally got him trained.'

Something in Lucas's heart twisted, unleashing the raft of feelings he'd been trying to keep at bay all day. The reaction went well beyond the parameters of witnessing a lovely moment. It was a combination of loss and hope. Loss that he'd never share that sort of exchange with Lily, and hope that—

He cut the thought off. He'd been an absolute idiot this morning. He'd seen Kiara plain as day in Reception, and when he'd had a chance to extend some sort of olive branch to her he'd stuck his foot in it.

Christmas isn't really my thing.

What had he been thinking?

No prizes for answering that. He hadn't. From the moment he'd woken up he'd stopped thinking, and his body had gone into the mode it had been in during Lily's final months: simply reacting.

Holding Kiara in his arms, smelling the soft perfume of her shampoo as her hair tickled his chin and his chest, feeling safe and warm and part of something bigger than himself—all that had awakened something in him he'd thought he'd left in the past. Happiness.

He'd felt happiness. Pure, wonderful, undiluted happiness. It hadn't been frantic, or wild, or just beyond his reach. It had been right there in his arms and it had smelt of cloves and cinnamon sugar and mint. And its name had been Kiara.

As soon as the sensation had registered, the guilt had poured in.

He'd never imagined himself feeling that way again. At peace with someone. As if he were part of a team. A future. And yet there he'd been, less than three years after his wife had died in his arms, holding another woman and never wanting the moment to come to an end.

The realisation had savaged him.

It was nothing to do with Kiara. Well… It was everything to do with Kiara. Or, more accurately, with his reaction to her. His feelings for her. The fact he'd wanted nothing more than to make love to her last night and had done so without a thought for how he might feel in the morning.

She was entirely faultless in this. It was one hundred percent him, and the fact that he'd never imagined caring for someone in that way ever again. He'd not known what to do with the new raft of feelings. Happiness. Contentment. Actual joy.

Feelings that had slammed up against his past so hard and fast he'd barely been able to breathe.

He'd had everything he'd ever wanted with Lily, and then she'd been taken away from him. In such a cruel way.

Harry hadn't been old enough to know the loss, but now he was. He adored Kiara. Loved everything about her. When he was with her, he glowed with happiness. He couldn't risk his son experiencing the level of loss Lucas had when he'd lost Lily. Not that Kiara was sick—but you simply didn't know, did you? Anything could happen. Sickness. Car crashes. Freak weather events. .

His mind had run wild with the thousands of reasons a man could end up standing at a graveside with nothing but a pathetic flower in his hand. A paltry show of feeling for a love that had been his life force. He didn't know how to love someone without loving them completely. With his whole being. Body. Heart. Soul.

Burying Lily had been like burying a part of himself. Even considering the possibility of experiencing that level of loss again was driving large wedges of ice straight into his heart. Fear. Panic. Confusion. Pain. Each one darker than the next to the point where he'd been completely and utterly panicked, convincing himself that his future had already been laid out for him.

He'd been so certain that his future was with Lily and life had showed him otherwise. He didn't know anything. He was destined to be alone. The perfection he'd shared with Kiara was not his to take. Not with what she'd already been through with her ex. What he'd been through with his wife. He was in no place to make promises for the future when he knew first-hand that the future was not in his control.

So he'd left. Convinced himself that he was doing it for Harry. That if, perchance, his son had found him with Kiara it would have confused things. And now here he was, face to face with a couple who, by the look of things, had enjoyed forty-seven years of marriage and were still smiling.

'What's your secret?' Lucas asked.

'For a good mince pie?' Mrs Thomas asked.

'What's that?' Mr Thomas leant in closer to his wife.

'He wants to know what my secret for a good mince pie is, Harold!'

They shared a look, then began to cackle. Low at first. Then building to a high fever-pitch of giggles.

'She buys them, lad! She buys 'em down the shops and pretends they're home-made.'

They laughed until they wiped tears away, and once again Lucas was struck by how wonderful their companionship seemed.

Multifaceted, and at its very core a deep well of love.

'I meant the secret of your marriage,' Lucas persisted. He'd take any advice he could get. Living his life half in the past and half in the present wasn't working. He had to find a way to go forward—only he didn't know how. 'What's the secret to staying so happily married?'

'Agree with everything she says,' Mr Thomas said, still laughing, and then putting on a placating voice. 'Yes, dear. That's right, dear. Anything you say, dear…'

Mrs Thomas swatted at him. 'If only it was that easy.' She leant forward and said conspiratorially, 'You'll not even come close to guessing the tricks I'll have to play to get him through these antibiotics. He's stubborn as a mule, he is. I had to promise him a steak pie tonight just to get him to come and see you.'

'That's just because I wanted steak pie!' Mr Thomas gave his wife a little tickle, then sobered as he turned back to Lucas. 'The real reason I came is because I want to make sure I'm around as long as she is. Drives me bonkers with all her energy—but, by God, it doesn't half keep me going. Wouldn't have lived a day of my life without this woman.

Worth her weight in gold, she is.' He leant forward and in a stage-whisper said, 'The real secret is making it clear to everyone around you that you won the lottery the day she agreed to marry you.'

The look Mrs Thomas gave her husband was so tender and full of love it nearly broke Lucas in two. He'd thought he was on track to have what they shared years back, when he'd asked Lily to marry him, but life had moved the goal posts for all of them. Lily, Harry and himself. And now, because of his poor behaviour this morning, for Kiara.

He had destroyed the very beginnings of something without even giving it a chance.

He had no idea how to shift the course of his own path to cross with Kiara's. Perhaps that had been the problem. Their fleeting connection had been a lesson to him to exercise more caution. Show more care. And never, ever again to hurt a woman who'd been so open, sharing with him her deepest humiliation only to feel it again by his own hand.

He owed her an apology. But words weren't going to be enough. The old saying was right. Actions did speak louder than words. And he had to make sure he was matching whatever apology he made to his intentions.

Until he knew what those were he was right back where he'd begun. Caught between his past and the present, not knowing which way to turn.

When Kiara opened the door for her next patient, Catrina, she was shocked to see Lucas, chatting away with her.

Not so much because it was weird for a GP to be speaking to a patient, but because it was weird for him to be outside a door he knew she'd be opening when he'd made it crystal-clear yesterday that he wanted nothing more to do with her.

She ran her thumb along the jagged remains of her festively decorated fingernails...all nibbled down yesterday.

He hadn't been *that* awful.

Despite her nerve-endings still burning like a bee sting, she had to concede that he hadn't cold-shouldered her or anything. He obviously just didn't want what had happened between them to happen again. Or, if he did, he wanted it to be between them. A secret. And if there was one thing she'd promised herself when she left London it was that she'd never again let someone treat her the way her ex had. As a secret.

'Hey, Kiara.' His grey eyes met hers. 'All right?'

'Fine, thanks,' she chirped, although the subtext was clear: *No thanks to you.* 'Catrina! So lovely to see you. Gosh… The twenty-eight-week appointment! If I didn't have it right here in black and white, I wouldn't have believed it from the size of you.'

'I know!' Catrina ran a hand over her neat bump then grinned, 'But look at me from the side!' She turned and jutted out her belly—which, to be fair, did look bigger from that angle.

Lucas hadn't moved a centimetre during this exchange and Kiara could feel him watching her. Was he inspecting her to see how she really was? Well, tough.

'Excellent.' She flicked her eyes to his and then to her patient's. 'Shall we get you out of the corridor and talk privately?'

It would be obvious that she didn't want him there, but she couldn't help it. Her response to Lucas was visceral. She wanted to touch him. Smell him. Taste him again. But wanting all those things rose like bile in her throat as she remembered his expression when he'd first laid eyes on her the morning after they'd had sex.

It might have been subconscious, but she'd

seen the way he'd pulled Harry just that little bit closer to him, hunched his shoulders that extra centimetre lower... Small but unmistakeable visual cues that had told her he thought he'd made a mistake. That moment had shot her straight back to the day she'd cheerfully answered her phone and listened with dawning understanding as an unfamiliar female voice had informed her that her 'boyfriend' had a wife and children.

She'd never felt more humiliated and ashamed.

And that doubled the pain. Because she knew in her heart that Lucas wasn't anything like her ex.

Peter had been a self-serving, duplicitous married man with a God complex.

Lucas was a widower with the kindest, most gentle spirit. A protective father who'd taken his very first steps into having a relationship. Not to mention the best kisser she'd ever met.

She squashed the physical response that came with those memories and forced herself to be practical.

Deep down, she knew he wasn't the sort of man to go around kissing people willy-nilly. Or to blank them the next day. They'd had a connection. He'd acted on it. Then he'd realised he'd made a mistake.

Perhaps the simplest explanation as to how they'd ended up in bed the other night was that they'd both had too heavy a dose of Christmas magic. But that somehow made it hurt that much more. Being someone's mistake.

Catrina, who was standing and waiting to go into the room, but couldn't because Kiara still hadn't moved, gave her an inquisitive look. 'Everything all right?'

Kiara popped on a chirpy smile she knew didn't reach her eyes. With a level of defiance she knew would travel all the way to the tall, dark and handsome GP whose eyes were glued to her, she said, 'Fine. Never been better. Sorry… I should be asking you if you're all right. Okay, then…away we go.'

Kiara stood to one side to let Catrina enter the room and, despite trying not to, looked at Lucas as she pulled the door shut.

There was something in those grey eyes of his she couldn't read. Remorse? An apology? She didn't know. Whatever it was, she didn't want it anywhere near her. She couldn't go down that road again. No matter how much of her heart she'd already lost to him. She'd simply have to soldier on until she grew yet more scar tissue.

And with a simple click of the door she promised herself that that would be that.

But of course it wasn't.

A few hours later she was on the phone to both of her parents, in a video call so they could witness her ugly crying in High Definition. She told them everything. About Lucas and Harry and how she'd fallen for them both. About how much she'd enjoyed doing all the festive events with them. About how things had gone further with Lucas but that it had obviously been a step too far for him. Whether it was because he was a widower or because she just hadn't been a good fit, she didn't know, but it had brought up all sorts of feelings and memories, and she'd thought she should tell them everything.

They sat silently, compassionately, and listened as she told them about Peter. About how he'd courted her. Wined and dined her straight into her own bed. Occasionally a hotel bed. But never his. Until, three years later, she'd found out why.

Her parents were shocked, but not disappointed in her as she'd expected. They comforted her, and called him a scoundrel and a rake and a couple of other words she hadn't realised her parents knew, and eventually her tears began to dry.

'Would you like to come home for Christmas, love?' her mum asked.

She had to admit she was tempted. To have hot water bottles magically appear in her childhood bed each night. To have that wonderful mish-mash of Indian cuisine from her mother's childhood and English from her father's on the Christmas dinner table after hours of laughter and fun in the family kitchen. Board games. Sentimental films.

But the idea of leaving her cottage—her new home—made her feel worse. As if 'The Incident' with Lucas, as she was now calling it, was driving her out of the new life she'd carved out for herself here in Carey Cove. Leaving, she realised, would be the worst thing she could do.

'I think I'll stay here,' she said.

'We can always come down to you, you know.'

Her spirits brightened at that. And without her having to say a word, her parents began to plan. Her father pulled a notebook on to the kitchen table as her mother rattled off a long list of things they mustn't forget to bring.

Before she knew it, Kiara was laughing.

'They have shops here in Cornwall, you know, Mum.'

Her mother feigned shock, then laughed as well. 'You know, love, we're more than happy to come. We want to come. But if you happen to chat to your young man and…you know…decide you'd like to celebrate Christmas in a different way, we're happy to go with whatever decision you make.'

Kiara scrunched her nose, feeling the sting of tears surfacing again. 'Thanks, Mum. But I think it'll be just us Baxters opening presents around the Christmas tree this year.'

They chatted a bit more, then said their goodbyes. Wanting to recapture a bit of the Christmas magic she'd lost over the past twenty-four hours, she went and got her duvet and made a little nest for herself on the sofa. She put on a Christmas film—the kind where brand-new work colleagues turned out to be princes from far-off kingdoms—and snuggled in for the evening.

A bit of fiction never hurt a girl. Especially at this time of year.

'I can't get any of the candy canes to stick!' Harry dropped the red and white striped sweets onto the table and folded his arms across his chest in a disgruntled huff.

'Come on, Harry. You said you wanted to decorate a gingerbread house.'

Lucas picked up a candy cane, squirted some of the white icing onto it, as the woman leading the workshop had instructed, and then, lacking the will even to try, ate it in one go.

'Can I have one?' Harry said, his lower lip beginning to tremble.

'Sure.' Lucas took another candy cane out of its protective wrapping and handed it to him.

'No! With icing on it, like you had!'

Lucas didn't fight it. He did as his son instructed and together they sat, side by side, amidst tables full of happy families merrily constructing gingerbread houses out of every sweetie known to mankind.

Lucas watched as Harry chomped and then swallowed his minty treat without so much as a glimmer of a smile. It wasn't top parenting. It wasn't even top adulting. Lucas knew he sounded as dispirited as his son.

Harry looked up at him, his big grey eyes a reflection of his own, his blond curls an echo of his mother's. 'I thought Kiara was going to be here.'

Lucas had too. And to be honest he was doing a terrible job of keeping up his part of the bargain: playing along. 'C'mon, son. She can't be with us for all our outings.'

'Why not?'

There were myriad reasons she couldn't accompany them absolutely everywhere, but the number one reason she wasn't here right now was because of the way Lucas had behaved. He'd panicked, and it had come across as cruel. He'd dug a hole for himself he didn't know how to get out of—because the truth was he didn't have the answers. He'd never been a widower before. Never fallen for anyone other than Lily...

He closed his eyes and instantly saw Kiara's expression when she'd found him bundling up a half-asleep Harry and listened to him muttering nonsense about getting him home for uniform and the right socks. It had been ridiculous and she'd known it. Of course Harry had needed those things, but usually a good parent would wait until their child had had a full night's sleep before taking them out of their girlfriend's—

The thought caught him up. He'd been thinking a lot of things about Kiara over the past couple of days. Thousands of them. How kind she was. How generous. Thoughtful, beautiful, strong... The list went on. But he'd never once thought of her as his *girlfriend*.

Was that what she'd become to him? It wasn't as if he was a Jack the Lad, jumping into bed with every woman who took his fancy. He'd not actually been with or wanted to be with anyone until Kiara had lit up his life—*their* lives—both literally and figuratively.

'It's not as much fun without Kiara,' Harry said mournfully.

'You're right,' Lucas conceded. 'It's not.'

And he'd pulled the plug on the possibility of Kiara being with them ever again. The way he'd treated her, he deserved the icy glances she'd been sending his way. But he simply didn't know how to come back from that. Not after what she'd been through.

He forced himself to try and look enthused about the unadorned gingerbread house sitting in front of them. 'But she couldn't make it today, so what do you say we make the best of it, eh? How about these chocolate buttons? Should we try putting some on the roof?'

Harry looked at the buttons and then up at his father, tears welling in his eyes. 'Why didn't we go past Mistletoe Cottage today?'

Another good question with a host of bad answers.

'I—' Lucas began, and then, not knowing how to explain to his son how he was feeling torn between his past and a future that felt as if it would betray the past, he began eating the chocolate buttons that were meant to be tiling the gingerbread house neither of them had any interest in.

'Daddy?' Harry tugged his father's arm. 'I want to see Mistletoe Cottage.'

Lucas's heart felt punctured by the request, because he knew the subtext. Harry wanted to see Kiara. And so did he. The days weren't as nice without her. Not as bright. They were certainly bereft of any Christmas spirit. But if they went past the cottage there was every chance they would run into Kiara, and he simply didn't know how to put into words what he felt.

He dropped a kiss on top of his son's head and pulled him in for a hug. Sitting here being more miserable wasn't helping anyone. 'What do you say we go out to the harbour and see if we can get a glimpse of her house from there?'

It wasn't the perfect solution, but if they walked out on to the quay Lucas was pretty sure Kiara's spectacularly decorated house would be shining away, a beacon for all who could see it.

They bundled up, and after making their excuses to the woman hosting the gingerbread-house-making went down to the harbour.

'Daddy?' Harry gave Lucas's hand a tug.
'Yes, son?'

'Why did you tell the lady I wasn't feeling well?'

'Ah, well...' Crikey. Now he was going to have to explain about white lies. Tonight was going down as an epic fail in the parenting department.

'Is it because we don't feel like smiling when Kiara's not here?'

The question pierced straight through his heart. He stopped where they were and dropped down so that he was face to face with his son. 'Hey... Hey, bud. Do you feel that sad without her?'

Harry nodded. 'And you do, too, Daddy.'

Lucas frowned, humbled by his son's observation and how accurate it was. He didn't feel good without Kiara. In fact, he felt downright miserable.

A thought suddenly broke through the fug of gloom he'd been wandering around in for the past couple of days. Was he paying a penance for loss that he had never actually owed? Lily had been clear with him. He wasn't to hold back from life. Not for her. Or for Harry. More to the point, he was to live life to the fullest *for* Harry. Living life mired in the past was something she had never wanted for her son. Or for Lucas.

Harry took his index fingers and put each one on the edges of Lucas's lips, first pushing them up, then down, as he said, 'When we're with her we smile, and when we're not all we want to do is be with her.'

Lucas sat back on his heels and looked at his wise three-year-old. That was pretty much it in a nutshell.

'Do you—' he began, and then stopped as a swell of emotion hitched in his throat.

He was about to ask his son a big question, and putting it into words felt as powerful as pulling his own heart out of his chest and asking for advice on how to go forward. How to live their lives.

'Would it be all right if—' Again the question caught in his throat.

How did you ask your child if it was all right to date someone who might possibly never want to see him again? Particularly when that little boy had never really known his mother's love. Two women loved Harry. Only one of them was here, up in that thatched-roofed, ornament-laden, fairy-lit testament to joy.

This was the decision Lily had wanted him

to make. Accepting the joy. Loving another woman wasn't about forgetting his past. It was being grateful for it and then, with care, being willing to open his heart to yet more love. More joy. More happiness.

He no longer battled the emotion bursting in his chest. 'You know your mummy loved you very much, don't you?' he said.

Harry nodded, then pointed at his heart. 'That's why she lives here.'

'Yes. Yes, that's right. And if I were to ask Kiara to spend a bit more time with us—'

Harry beamed and clapped his hands, 'You mean a *lot* more time with us?'

Lucas wiped away a couple tears of his own and said, 'Hopefully. If Daddy hasn't mucked it up.'

Harry's little eyebrows drew together and he asked, 'Did you tell Kiara we weren't feeling well, too?'

Lucas had to laugh. 'Something like that. And now we have to find a way to let her know we're feeling better and that we'd love to see her again.'

A fresh burst of energy sent an empowering charge through his entire body. He rose and took his son's hand in his.

'C'mon, Harry. Daddy's got an idea. Shall we go and see if we can make it work?'

His son's cheers were all the encouragement he needed.

CHAPTER ELEVEN

KIARA'S NEWEST PATIENT and friend, Liane, was glowing with excitement. And it wasn't just her baby she was excited about. Kiara was about to unveil yet more decorations for her house, as it was now only forty more sleeps until Christmas.

Not that she was counting.

She was absolutely counting.

'Honestly,' Liane said to Kiara. 'This is the absolute best Christmas I've ever had. The whole of Carey Cove thinks so, if I'm honest. Will you be doing this every year?'

Kiara made an indeterminate gesture that she hoped said *Sure!* And also *There are no guarantees in life!* What she really wanted to say was *Absolutely, yes, but my heart's not in it nearly as much as it was back when Lucas and Harry were—*

She cut the thought short. Lucas and Harry weren't anything any more, apart from Lucas-and-Harry-shaped holes in her heart. As much as she wanted it to be otherwise, it simply wasn't to be.

She'd never been more grateful for a weekend in her life! It wasn't so much that she wanted to avoid Lucas… Well… She *did* want to avoid Lucas, because no matter how hard she tried she still couldn't shake the feeling that there was something unfinished between them. Just as there was that mysterious *something* missing from her home's over-the-top decorations which, like the final piece of a puzzle, would make it perfectly perfect.

'C'mon!' Liane rubbed her hands together, clearly beginning to feel the cold of the crisp, bright winter's day. 'I'm going to turn into an icicle if you don't choose soon.'

'I can't choose!'

Kiara's face stretched into a helpless expression. If this had been three days ago she knew who would be choosing. Harry. She swallowed back the lump of emotion and brightened her tone.

'You choose. Which one?' Kiara held up a star and then an angel.

'The angel, for sure.' Liane's grin widened. 'She looks just like you.'

'Ha!' Kiara smirked, holding up the blonde,

blue-eyed archetypal angel and then giving her dark ponytail a flick. 'Maybe if I did this...' She lifted the angel above her head and struck a beatific pose, then, as she looked at her new friend, realised she was properly freezing. 'Wait there!'

She ran into the house and grabbed a cosy blanket off the back of the sofa, desperately trying not to remember the last time she'd been on it, her limbs tangled with a certain tall, dark and handsome GP.

She ran back, flicked the blanket out to its full length and wrapped it round Liane's shoulders. 'There you are. Got to keep you and your little one cosy.'

Liane laughed, said thank you, and then, as she pulled the blanket close, her expression turned earnest. 'Seriously, Kiara. I mean it. I know you're my midwife, and all, and that we haven't known each other that long, but I hope you know I count you as a friend. I mean—you're amazing. You achieve big things in small amounts of time.'

Like falling in love with the one man she shouldn't? Yup. She'd certainly done that straight away. Tick! Done and dusted.

'Hardly,' she said, instead of pouring her heart out to her new friend and telling her about everything the way she'd done with her parents. With Lucas. The pain she had tried to keep at bay was threatening to burst through her mental blocks. This moment was proof that she didn't have to rely on Lucas for friendship.

Liane held her hands out wide. 'Look at what you've done in the last two weeks! I haven't managed to do anywhere near the same in ten years of living here! I hope you stay. I hope you stay for ever and we grow up to be old ladies in wheelchairs, admiring Carey Cove's famous Christmas lights at Mistletoe Cottage.'

Kiara pressed her hands to her heart, truly touched and then she said, more mischievously, 'When we're that old we'll have to hire some strapping young men to put up all the decorations!'

'Ooh…' Liane's eyes lit up. 'Why wait until we're old? We could hire some now.' She suddenly pulled a face. 'Do you think my husband would mind?' And then she burst out in hysterical laughter, pretending to be in a panic that he might have heard. 'Aw… Bless… He's the best-looking man in the village for me—and that's what counts, isn't it?'

Kiara nodded, absorbing the sight of her friend's face turning soft with affection as she no doubt conjured an image of her husband wearing a tool belt or possibly nothing, while her own thoughts instantly pinged to the man she would happily have as her Mr January through to December if she could. But she couldn't.

'I guess we'll have to leave it until we're older, then, before getting some young men to put up the rooftop decorations.'

They both looked up to the roof, no doubt imagining entirely different men up there, doing alpha male things in various stages of undress.

'And I guess I'd better get back and make tonight's tea.' With a small, contented sigh, Liane began to fold up the blanket Kiara had handed her, and then she asked, more seriously, 'Do you have any more decorations you want putting in awkward places? I'm happy to ask Gavin if you need me to. He's not brilliant at DIY, but he is happy to give things a go.'

Kiara did want more decorations, but she just couldn't put her finger on what was missing. She looked up at Santa on the roof of the cottage. He was by the chimney, posed to look as if he was about to climb down with a big bag of presents. The orange and red glow of the sunset was disappearing in the sky, and the lights she had strung like rows of icing along the house were beginning to offer their warm glow to the fast-approaching darkness. She heard jingle bells and smiled. Christmas really had gone to her head!

'Did you hear that?' Liane asked, cocking her head to the side. 'Are those...*jingle* bells?'

Kiara started. So it hadn't just been her. She tilted her head to one side, as if that might be the best way to hear something better, and, yes... It was faint, but there was the unmistakably cheery sound of jingle bells rising up from the main road at the port. The way the road was angled made it possible to see whoever was coming once the vehicle came round the first bend.

'It must be someone with bells attached to their car,' Kiara said, feeling a shot of festive adrenaline spiking through her.

'No...' Liane's voice was awe-filled. 'It so much better than that.'

Kiara couldn't even speak and agree. Liane was right. It was a million times better than that.

It was Lucas. And Harry. On top of a flat-bed truck that was somehow transporting the most beautiful sleigh with a full complement of reindeer hitched to the front.

How he'd found a sleigh—glittering and twinkling in the approaching darkness—let alone reindeer tame enough to be hitched to a sleigh with full swags of jingle bells was beyond her. She felt as if she was in the middle of a Christmas miracle.

She clearly wasn't alone. She could see front doors being flung open and children and adults alike running out into their gardens to cheer and sing snippets of Christmas songs as the enormous truck—bedecked in fairy lights, no less—slowly worked its way up the hill until, with a great sense of purpose, it came to a halt right in front of Mistletoe Cottage.

Lucas and Harry were in the driver's seat of the sleigh. Harry was bouncing all over the place, waving and pretending to steer the reindeer, and generally enjoying being the centre of attention, but it was Lucas Kiara was watching... Because his eyes—his entire energy—was solely on her.

She felt his gaze as if it were a sparkling Christmas elixir...magic from a fairy godmother's wand. Only he was no godmother, and the look in those grey eyes of his would enchant her for ever. He cared for her. She could see it now. And, more importantly, she could feel it. For Lucas, a hugely private man who'd endured so much emotional turmoil over the past few years, to make such an enormous, public, *festive* show of affection meant only one thing: he was falling in love every bit as much as she was.

What they'd shared was now the opposite of a secret. It was out there for the whole of Carey Cove to see.

The only question was…could she trust it?

Before an ounce of doubt that the gesture was genuine could creep in, Harry was out of the sleigh and clambering down onto the flatbed, where an obliging neighbour swung him off as he cried, 'Kiara! Kiara!'

Her heart filled to bursting as he ran and leapt up into her arms as if they'd been parted for an eternity. She buried her head in his little-boy scent as he wrapped his arms round her neck. He smelt of Christmas trees and cloves and winter mint. He smelt of love.

Eventually, he pulled back and asked, 'Do you like it?'

'I love it,' she answered honestly, as the pair of them turned and looked up at the sleigh where Lucas, still aboard, was looking down at the pair of them.

As their eyes met, her heart near enough

exploded. His expression was a charged mix of hope and concern. Affection and intent. She could tell he wanted to talk, and she did, too… But it appeared having a sleigh arrive in front of her house warranted action, not a quiet conversation by the fire with a cup of hot chocolate which was what she really wanted.

Lucas was charged for action…and yet standing up here on the flatbed, watching his son run into his girlfriend's arms—for that was what Kiara was to him if she'd forgive him—made him feel more complete than he'd felt in years.

Everything about this moment was unbelievably outside the box for him. Making a gesture so epic, not only to show Kiara he knew he'd made a mistake, but that he cared for her, was definitely not in the emotional toolbox he'd left home with when he'd set off for medical school all those years ago. Life had changed him. He now knew how precious it was. How foolish it was to let fear and pride make decisions for him when really, all along, he should have been listening to his heart.

He wanted to go to her, pull her into his arms and whisper apologies, tell her how much she'd changed his perspective on both life and love, but it seemed when you drove a sleigh and reindeer up to the home of the woman you hoped loved you as much as you loved her, you weren't the star attraction. The sleigh and the reindeer were.

The whole of Carey Cove appeared to have gathered outside Mistletoe Cottage and somehow, magically—Kiara would definitely have said magically—everything began to move into place as if the entire thing had been planned.

Kiara's little red car was relocated to a neighbour's drive. The snowmen were rearranged. The dancing penguins were put into action, wiggling their little animatronic bums as if they, too, had been waiting for the sleigh and reindeer to appear.

Davy Trewelyn, the publican, a tall, portly, white-bearded man, turned up with a 'Ho-ho-ho!' in a perfect Santa suit. And his wife, the rosy-cheeked and ever-smiling Darleen, showed up in a Mrs Claus outfit complete with a huge tray of gingerbread men.

The village's children were beside themselves, but between the schoolteachers, the firemen, the local bobby and, of course, the parents, who had all gathered to see Santa's sleigh and reindeer, a jolly kind of order was formed out of the chaos.

The sleigh and reindeer were unloaded and set up in Kiara's drive, flanked by a row of living Christmas trees, lined up in red pots and each decorated with a whorl of fairy lights and topped alternately with stars and angels. But there was only one true angel in his eyes: Kiara Baxter. The woman who had touched his life in a way he hadn't thought possible.

He kept trying to get to her, but across a fence of jumbo candy canes they shared a look of mutual understanding: their talk would have to wait.

Eventually, when the reindeer had had their fill of carrots and Mr and Mrs Claus needed to go back to their 'day jobs' at the pub, and the children's tummies began to grumble for their suppers, the crowd began to thin.

One of the mums from the local playgroup asked Lucas in a knowing tone if Harry would like to come to supper at theirs. 'It's spaghetti tonight, and bowls of vanilla ice cream for afters. Nothing fancy, but—'

'Spaghetti's great,' Lucas said, not even looking at her.

His eyes had been glued to Kiara all night

and, as if they'd been sharing the same enriched pool of energy, hers had been locked on his. Except for this exact moment now, when his son was barrelling into her for another hug.

The look on their faces as they wrapped their arms around each other made him feel as if his thirst was being quenched with a life-affirming soul juice. As they waved goodbye to each other, and promised to see one another soon, it was as if a multicoloured aura surrounded them. One made up of hues of pure joy, contentment and peace. That Christmas song about peace on earth came to him, and in a moment's stillness he caught himself mouthing the words, about how the place love and harmony had to come from was within.

That was when he knew. Straight down to his marrow he knew he was in love with Kiara. And if she would have him, she was his future.

He reduced the space between them in a few long-legged strides and pulled her into his arms. She didn't push him away or demand an explanation. She just held him, and their bodies exchanged energy, heartbeats. When at long last, arms still wrapped round each other's waist, they pulled back to look at one another, Lucas knew she felt the same way, too.

Not even caring about the wolf whistles the few remaining Carey Covers were sending their way, he kissed her. By the time they parted there was no one else around. It was as if they'd been left in a snow globe entirely of Kiara's creation. And he loved being a part of it.

'Are the reindeer going to be all right?'

Lucas grinned, turning her so that his arms were still around her, but his chin was resting on her silky hair, her ponytail tickling his neck. They watched as the reindeer dug into the bags of hay they'd been left.

'The owner is coming to collect them soon. They'll be back with their manger tonight.'

Kiara twisted herself so that she could shoot him one of her trademark cheeky grins. 'Their manger, eh? I thought you were immune to Christmas magic.'

'Not with you in my life.'

She pulled back then, and asked the question he'd seen in her eyes all night. 'Am I in your life? Is that what you want?'

He nodded, and then gestured towards her cottage. 'Shall we go in? I can grovel inside so you don't freeze to death.'

She laughed and blew out a little cloud of mist, as if to affirm that inside would definitely be a better choice. Then she hesitated a moment. 'Grovelling won't be necessary, but...' her top tooth captured her lower lip for a moment as she sought and found the best word-choice '...honesty will. One hundred percent honesty, okay?'

He crossed his heart and held up his hand in a Boy Scout's salute. 'I promise nothing less.' He flattened his hand against his heart. 'I owe you nothing less.'

'You don't owe me anything, Lucas. That's the point.'

She didn't sound angry or vindictive. She sounded determined. Resolute. As if she was showing him where she'd set her moral compass and it was up to him if he was on the same trajectory as her.

He let her comment hit its mark and then settle as they went into the house. She excused herself to make some warm drinks, assigning him the task of lighting a fire. As he went about making a pile of kindling and putting the logs in just the right place, he realised she was absolutely right. A relationship wasn't about obligation. It was about choice. And he chose loving Kiara over not loving her.

When they were settled on the sofa, a fire crackling away in the fireplace and warm mugs of hot chocolate complete with marshmallows in their hands, he took a sip, then set down his mug and turned to her.

'First and foremost, I would like to offer you an apology for my behaviour the other day.'

Kiara nodded, neither refusing nor accepting his apology. She was waiting for the explanation.

'You're the first woman I've felt like this about since...'

'Since Lily,' she filled in for him. 'She's not a secret, Lucas. She's part of who you are. Part of who Harry is.'

It was a generous gesture. Openly acknowledging the woman he'd loved and then lost to a terrible disease. The woman who had given him Harry. A boy without whose energy and verve he might not have survived her loss as emotionally intact as he was.

'I thought I'd finished grieving for her.' He raked a hand through his hair and gave the back of his neck a rub. 'Meeting you taught me I still had another step to take.'

She nodded, openly and actively listening.

He gave a little laugh. 'I actually needed to take her advice. She wanted this...' He moved his hand between the two of them. 'For me to fall in love again.'

Kiara's breath hitched in her throat. 'Is that what's happening?'

Lucas gave a proper laugh now. 'It's what's *happened*! I'm in love with you, Kiara Baxter.'

'But...?' She said it without malice, but she was still waiting for her explanation and she was right. He owed her the truth.

'At first I thought it was betraying Lily to love another woman the way I love you. But then...' His breath grew shaky as he rubbed his hand against the nape of his neck once more. 'The truth was I was scared. Loving someone—loving *you* the way I do... I can't do it half-heartedly and that frightened me. I didn't want to lose sight of myself the way I did before. But I realised fear and vulnerability are all part of loving someone. Love isn't about limits. It's about opening up. Expanding your heart, not blocking it off.'

He stroked the backs of his fingers along her cheek.

'It's about being brave with someone. Trusting someone enough to believe that whatever you do, no matter how frightening, it'll be so much better facing those things together. I want to be brave with you.' He pressed his hands to his heart. 'You've made me realise my heart has a much greater capacity for love and resilience than I thought. Harry adores you. I adore you. I mean...' He held his hands out wide. 'If you can get *me* to enjoy *Christmas* you're obviously a miracle-worker.'

Kiara was smiling now, and laughing, and crying, and moving across the sofa to climb onto his lap and receive the kisses he was so hungry to give her.

After a few moments she pulled back, and without words began to trace her fingers along his face. His forehead, his cheekbones, his nose and chin. As if she were memorising him. As if she was finally believing that she didn't need permission to love him—she just needed to love him. And that was when it hit him. She had been every bit as frightened as he was.

'It takes courage, doesn't it?' he asked. 'To love after being so badly hurt.'

She nodded, and he saw a swell of emotion rushing through her eyes. 'It does.' She scrunched her nose and gave it a wriggle. 'I guess after you left I felt as if my future was destined to always be somebody's secret, and I didn't want that.'

'I hate it that I made you feel that way.'

Again, she scrunched her nose. 'The way you left did hurt me, but really I think I'm the one who made myself feel that way. I could've called you on it then and there. I knew in my heart you weren't a "love 'em and leave 'em" kind of guy, and that there had to be something else going on, but I let my past experience colour how I responded.'

'Hey…' He ran his fingers through a lock of her hair, then brushed her cheek with his fingers. 'I made a bad call. I was scared and I acted like an idiot, and that behaviour triggered the fears and hurt embedded in you. It was a not-so-perfect storm.'

'One that's blown over?'

'One that's definitely blown over,' he confirmed solidly.

'Should we seal that with a kiss?'

A smile teased at the corners of her lips, and then blossomed into a full-blown grin as he tugged her in close to him again.

'I think we should seal it with a thousand kisses. Maybe more?'

She giggled and asked, 'Just how long do you think it's going to take Harry to eat some spaghetti and a scoop of ice cream?'

'Long enough for me to do this…' Lucas said, scooping her up and laying her out on the sofa where, smiling and laughing, they tangled their limbs together and enjoyed a good old-fashioned kissing session...as if they were teenagers.

And that was how he felt. Young again. Unweighted by a past that he didn't know how to move on from. Stronger for having Kiara in his life. For accepting and giving her love. Their strength united in loving his son.

This, he realised as the twinkle of the star atop her tree caught his eye, was the true meaning of Christmas. And he was excited to be celebrating it with a full heart for the rest of his life.

EPILOGUE

'WHO WANTS TO put the star on the Christmas tree?'

'Which one?' Harry and Kiara asked in tandem, instantly dissolving into fits of giggles.

Lucas pretended to look confused, and then rotated in a slow circle to see where not one, nor two, but seven full-sized Christmas trees circled the front garden, with five more to come. They'd decided their famous decorations—famous for Cornwall, anyway—should come with a new twist this year.

The first tree was covered in ornamental partridges made of every material imaginable. Felt, papier mâché, glass, plastic, wood… They were all decorations that visitors had brought to be part of the Mistletoe Cottage Merry Christmas Fest. Some of the decorations had been handmade by people of all different ages. One artisan glass blower had even made the tree-topper for that one. A robust, but beautifully ornamental partridge that glowed in the wintry sunlight.

Today, of course, was swans, and the tree glowed with all of the offerings from both near and far.

While the stream of visitors was steady, it still felt very much as if this was the same small local project that Kiara had begun in the name of charity. The fact that she'd been able to give First Steps healthy donations every year for the last few years on behalf of the wider community was just the icing on the gingerbread man.

But, more than that, now that Harry and Lucas had moved in Kiara's house no longer felt like her little cottage—it felt like a home. A family home for her, and Lucas, and Harry—whom she'd now officially adopted—and their latest addition, a precocial curtain-climbing kitten called Holly.

'Oof!' Kiara's hands flew to her tummy, extended to accommodate a thirty-seven-week pregnancy.

Lucas was by her side in an instant, putting Harry in charge of holding the star. 'Everything all right, love? Is it time?'

Kiara shook her head, although she was

uncertain if this was the real thing or not. 'You'd think with my experience I'd know!'

Lucas laughed and said, 'Remember Marnie? She said pretty much the same thing when her baby was due.'

Kiara nodded, breathing through a pain that was mixed with the pleasure of knowing their baby would be with them at Christmastime. She already had a list of Christmas-themed names she hoped Lucas would like. And Harry, of course.

He was hopping up and down, singing, 'Baby! Baby! I'm going to get a baby for Christmas!'

Lucas gave his son's head a playful rub and said, 'Yes, you are, son—but should we maybe get Kiara to the sofa, so she can have a rest before we figure out if we need to take her up to Carey House?'

Kiara grinned. 'I think the fact that we have a midwife "just popping in to see the decorations" on the hour every hour will probably stand us in good stead.'

'That's a good point. Do you want to ring Nya?'

They shared a smile. Nya was the one who'd had the very first inklings of their romance, and as such, when they'd found out Kiara was pregnant earlier this year, they'd thought it only fitting to ask if she'd be their midwife.

'I'll ring her when the next one— Oof!' Kiara flinched again.

Harry's eyes went wide. 'Daddy, quick! Get the sleigh to come! The one with the reindeer! Then we can *fly* Kiara to the hospital!'

Lucas gave him a hug, told him it was a great idea, and then pretended to think a minute before suggesting, 'Why don't you grab Kiara's bag and we'll go the normal way?'

'Walking?' Harry looked confused. 'Can she do that?'

'It's what every good midwife recommends,' Lucas said. 'I have that on good authority.' He tapped the side of his nose, then gave Kiara's cheek a kiss. 'Unless you want to kill me for saying as much and put you in the car like any normal panicked father?'

Kiara grinned, every bit as thrilled and panicked and having no more idea what to do than her 'men'.

'Walking's fine. It's a beautiful day.'

And it was. She gave her husband a kiss and then, because he looked as if he was feeling left out, dropped a kiss on Harry's forehead.

She loved being his parent, and a wife to his father. And she couldn't wait to have this baby so that they could all enjoy the Christmas season as one big happy family.

* * * * *